KINGS OF THE MOUNTAIN

MORGAN BRICE

ebook ISBN: 978-1-64795-003-3
Print ISBN: 978-1-64795-004-0

Cover art by Natania Barron
Darkwind Press is an imprint of DreamSpinner Communications, LLC

KINGS OF THE MOUNTAIN

By Morgan Brice

1

DAWSON

Dawson King walked off the jet bridge into the Asheville, North Carolina airport, closer to home than he had been in three years. He still wore the same camouflage fatigues that he'd had on when he left the Army base in Afghanistan, and everything he owned filled the worn duffel bag on his shoulder.

He looked around the terminal, taking in every detail of a "normal" civilian setting, something Dawson had dreamed about while deployed. The smell of hamburgers from the food court, the chatter of voices with familiar accents, and the signs written in a language he could read—all of it assured him that he was finally, permanently, home.

Four years of infantry training and combat, dangerous patrols, injuries, and near-death experiences had changed him. Dawson hadn't been a green recruit, not after having been raised in a monster-hunting dynasty and making his first kill at age ten. But it was one thing to shoot a werewolf or behead a vampire, and another thing entirely to be locked in a firefight with other human beings, kill-or-be-killed. He wasn't the same man who had run away from a problem he didn't know how to handle. But now, Dawson hoped his self-imposed exile was going to pay off.

He finally had the chance to make the life he dreamed of, with the man of his dreams. And he intended to make good on his promise to himself not to fuck it up.

Dawson picked up his pace. The Army didn't allow personal electronic devices in a hot zone. He had hoped to buy a cheap cell phone in an airport store during one of his many layovers, but between the flight changes and missed connections, he had barely managed to get himself onto the planes in time.

His stomach growled, reminding him that food was long overdue. Dawson had traveled through enough time zones that he had no idea what meal he ought to be hungry for. According to his watch, he'd gone backward in time more than nine hours from when he lifted off from the military airport; a long flight made even longer by the delays. Sleeping on the plane didn't work well, not when his six-foot-two-inch frame didn't fit in a cramped airline seat. He was jet-lagged enough to feel like he'd been out drinking, with a headache and scratchy throat from the dry cabin air.

None of that mattered. Dawson was finally home.

"Thank you for your service."

The speaker, another traveler, didn't slow for a response. Dawson had heard the same many times as he connected through civilian airports. He appreciated the sentiment, but despite his commendations and honorable discharge, Dawson didn't feel like a hero. He'd signed up to do a job, and he did it well. And if his superior marksmanship came from being trained to hunt creatures few people believed existed, well, Dawson had made sure the U.S. Army remained none the wiser.

He paused long enough to wolf down two hot dogs and an order of fries, hoping it would silence his growling stomach, then slurped a Coke, savoring the familiar tastes. Up ahead, he could see the exit from the security area. He grinned and felt his heartbeat speed up in anticipation.

Uncle Denny had promised to pick him up. He'd be waiting and maybe Grady, too. Grady, Dawson's best friend, favorite hunting partner, cousin, and now, maybe more.

Grady was still a King, even though not related by blood, since Grady's father, Aaron, had been adopted. *That makes it so much less complicated for the two of us.*

Dawson passed the security guard and walked into the regional airport's atrium, looking one way and then the other, but he didn't see Denny or Grady.

Maybe they went to get coffee. My flight was *late.* Still, Denny had all of Dawson's flight numbers and had assured him he would get alerts about any changes. He should have known about the delays. Dawson pushed away the worry that surfaced in the back of his mind. There were all kinds of reasons why Uncle Denny might be late.

Except that there really weren't. Not after Dawson had been gone for so long, and not after all the plans they'd made.

Something was wrong.

Dawson's combat senses shifted into high gear as he scanned the atrium once more. Compared to the huge international airports he'd flown through, Asheville didn't have many places a person could be overlooked. Dawson could see into the sundry stores and coffee shop, and his "welcome home" party was definitely AWOL. Memories of his latest nightmare surfaced, along with a prickle of worry in the back of his mind.

Do they even have payphones anymore? he wondered, figuring he'd need to find a customer service desk.

Just as Dawson scanned the overhead signs for a clue about which direction to head, the glass entranceway doors opened and a man jogged inside, looking worried like he might miss his flight. It took Dawson a moment to realize that he knew this man, hunted with him, trusted him with his life. His best friend, next to Grady.

Colt Summers wore a frantic expression as he did his own scan of the lobby, freezing when he spotted Dawson. The welcoming smile didn't reach his eyes, and Dawson now felt certain that something was not right.

"Daw! Good to see you, man. Glad you're home." Colt slapped him on the shoulder, pulled him into a quick bro hug, then stepped back.

"Good to be home," Dawson murmured. "Where's Uncle Denny?" *And Grady.*

Colt's smile dimmed. "They sent me instead. They're at home, waiting for you. Probably gonna whip my ass for running late." He glanced down, looking for luggage. "You got stuff at baggage claim?"

Dawson shook his head, playing along for now. "Nope. Just this one."

He wanted to ask a million questions and bit them back. They'd have a long car ride to talk. His stomach was tight, the way it got going into a mission—or heading out to hunt a ghoul or a wendigo. Dawson had depended on his instincts to survive for a long time, and he wasn't about to ignore the gut warning he felt now.

If it had been anyone else but Colt, he would have dug in his heels, refused to leave the airport until he knew what was going on. But he trusted Colt, and Uncle Denny knew that. If his uncle couldn't come himself, he knew Dawson would accept Colt as a substitute.

From the tension in Colt's shoulders, Dawson figured his friend knew he was in for an interrogation as soon as they got into the car.

Dawson couldn't help feeling another pang of disappointment when Colt led them to his black Ford F-150.

"You didn't drive the Mustang?" Dawson's red 1969 Boss 429 Mustang was his pride and joy, and it had come in handy outrunning the sheriff on more than one occasion when a hunt went wrong.

"Didn't figure you'd take kindly to anyone behind the wheel but you," Colt replied with a shadow of his usual grin. "Thought I'd let you two get reacquainted in private."

Dawson hoped he kept his wince hidden, as Colt's words hit a little too close to home. He had been planning a private reunion, one that was a long time coming, to set things right and make good on a promise. It wasn't with his car.

Colt's eyes widened just enough Dawson knew his friend registered the mistake. "Come on," he said. "We've still got a drive to get you where you need to go."

Dawson settled into the passenger seat, quiet as Colt navigated the airport parking exit and headed for the main road home. His cluttered thoughts and ricocheting emotions made him glad for a chance to collect himself.

The King family had named Cunanoon Mountain in Transylvania County, North Carolina, before the Revolutionary War, and staked out the land for a homestead and the village of Kingston. Then they got down to the business of hunting monsters, which had been their charge from the British king back in their native Wales.

Few noticed that "Cunanoon" was the sound-alike for *Cwn Annwn*, Welsh for hellhound.

Their neighbors brewed moonshine, and while the Kings didn't run stills of their own, they kept the werewolves away from the bootleggers. Most young men in the Carolina mountains honed their driving skills outrunning the revenuers during Prohibition. The King boys out-drove vampires.

Dawson's father and his two brothers inherited the King family legacy. His Uncle Denny never married, but he doted on his nephews like sons. Dawson's father, Ethan, had been the oldest. He and Dawson's mom had died in a plane crash when Dawson was seventeen. Aaron, the youngest of the brothers, was adopted. Aaron had always been treated like one of the family, and while the adoption wasn't a secret, nobody except Aaron ever seemed to care. Aaron had two sons, Grady and his older brother, Knox. They were both Kings, but not by blood.

Aaron had been ten when his parents died on a hunt. Robert King, Dawson's grandfather, had been good friends with Aaron's parents, and adopted the boy, loving him like his own. Ethan and Denny had accepted Aaron as a brother, making him welcome. But Aaron had always been insecure, feeling the need to prove himself, to show that he was a "real" King. No one else demanded that and efforts to reassure Aaron never seemed to get through. Fortunately, neither Grady nor Knox felt that burden, accepting that they were Kings of the heart, as well as by name.

Aaron's wife, Camille, had her fill of rural life and hunting even before Knox got sidelined by a bad fall while hunting a wraith. She divorced Aaron and went back to Asheville, a more "civilized" place, according to her. They never heard from her again.

Aaron and Grady often hunted together, but just as often, Grady hunted with Dawson from the time they were in their teens. Those were some of the best times in his life, Dawson recalled, smiling in spite of his worry. He and Grady had been fearless, reckless—and damn good at what they did.

Dawson was two years older than Grady. They were inseparable, partners in crime, hunting buddies, and brothers-by-another-mother. Dawson had never known anyone—before or since—who seemed to just "get" him on every level. The two of them were always in sync, finishing each other's sentences, sharing in-jokes, anticipating the other's moves.

Then Grady turned seventeen. And suddenly he wasn't the gawky, lanky kid-sidekick anymore. He grew into his shoulders, filled out, and seemed to delight in finding excuses to take his shirt off around Dawson whenever the opportunity presented itself.

Dawson had never hidden that he was gay from family and friends, but he'd usually gone off the mountain to scratch that particular itch. Early on, he and Colt had a friends-with-benefits arrangement, but that was years ago, and they'd long since decided that being just-friends suited them both. Grady hadn't made any declaration about his orientation, but more than once Dawson had caught Grady checking out a good-looking guy, so he had his suspicions.

The two years' age difference between them shouldn't have mattered, but it did to Dawson. Especially when he couldn't shake the feeling that Grady was flirting with him, intentionally trying to goad him into noticing. Grady'd always had a bit of hero worship in the way he looked at Dawson, and Dawson had always taken his responsibility seriously as the older of the two to protect Grady. Even from himself.

The longer they spent time on the road and on hunts together, the more Dawson felt a powerful attraction to Grady. He'd always been fond of the younger man, but Dawson found himself admiring the person Grady was growing into. Grady deserved to find the right guy

—if that's what he wanted—who could make him happy. And as much as Dawson wished fervently that could be him, he knew he couldn't take the chance that Grady might feel pressured or obligated to respond if Dawson made any advances.

Not to mention how Grady's mother had always carried on about how awful it was to marry a "cousin," something that she claimed no one in *her* family had ever done. She'd made her position loud and clear while she was married to Aaron, which had not endeared her to the rest of the community. Such marriages were legal in North Carolina, and not uncommon in the rural areas.

The fact that Grady wasn't a cousin by blood probably wouldn't matter to Camille. But what if Grady had accepted his mother's bias? Maybe Dawson had imagined the flirtation, or worse, projected his own feelings onto the other man. So Dawson took the edge off with hookups and out-of-town one-night stands, very aware that he tended to choose partners with a resemblance to Grady.

Until he couldn't stand it any longer.

That's when Dawson enlisted.

Once they were on the main highway, Dawson turned to watch Colt's profile.

"So...what happened with Uncle Denny and Grady?"

Colt's grip on the steering wheel tightened, and the tic in his jaw told Dawson that the other man didn't want to have this conversation. "They're both alive. But a hunt went wrong a week ago, and Grady isn't dealing with it very well."

A week, Dawson thought. That was when he'd stopped getting emails from Grady. He had tried to convince himself the silence was due to any number of impersonal reasons, but Dawson knew in his gut something wasn't right. His responses from Uncle Denny had gotten short and less frequent around the same time.

Was this what his nightmare had been warning him about?

"Could you be a little clearer?" Dawson knew Colt could read the warning in his tone.

"Grady got hurt. Aaron was killed. Grady's not dealing well with it. Uncle Denny didn't want to leave Grady alone. So they sent me."

Dawson's head swam. *Uncle Aaron, dead? That's hard to even imagine. He was always so full of life. And Grady—it's got to be bad if he couldn't come. Oh, God. I almost lost him. Plus there's something Colt isn't saying, something even worse. Because if Uncle Aaron died on a hunt, then Grady had to have been right there when it happened. That's bad, really bad. No one should see their parent die, especially not like that.*

Colt still didn't look at Dawson, and Dawson felt fear and anger roil in his belly, a reaction to the grief. "How about you tell me the whole damn truth, Colt? Why are you holding back?"

Colt sighed and seemed to deflate a little. "Because Uncle Denny wanted to tell you himself."

Dawson scrubbed a hand down over his face, struggling to rein in his temper. Scared to find out just how bad it was, and feeling guilty because he left for the Army, Dawson thought he might have a meltdown.

"Dude, you can't keep me hanging for over an hour until we get home. Please." Dawson didn't care about begging. He needed to know what had happened, so he could figure out what to do when he got there.

Colt slid him a sidelong glance and relented. "If I tell you, you've got to keep Uncle Denny from whupping my ass, because he told me not to."

"You know I will."

Colt tightened his grip on the wheel, his knuckles bone-white and kept his eyes on the road, a convenient way to avoid looking at Dawson. "We've had some problems with rogue werewolves and feral shifters lately. They like our neck of the woods because it's remote. If they didn't bother anyone, we might have let it ride. But there've been livestock kills and some attacks on people that just barely got pushed back."

"How did you know you've got weres *and* shifters?" Dawson fell back into hunting mode out of old habit.

"It's that time of the month," Colt replied with a smirk. "Seriously? The weres are only out the three days of the full moon. You know this shit—did you forget it all while you were gone?"

8

Dawson flinched. "Just confirming. Didn't want to assume."

"Wouldn't be the first time you made an 'ass' out of 'u' and 'me.'" Colt's smile faded. "Anyhow, we've all been out trying to track down one particular werewolf. He didn't stay in the forest and feed off the deer. If he had, no one would have bothered him. Kept coming near towns, snatching farm animals. Grady and Aaron thought they'd figured out a pattern and guessed where he'd strike next. So they did a stakeout."

Dawson found he was holding his breath. He had an awful feeling about how this was going to go.

"They were right," Colt continued, his voice flat. "The werewolf got the drop on Aaron. Grady shot the wolf—silver to the heart—but he'd already bit Aaron."

"Fuck."

"Aaron begged Grady to shoot him. Grady refused. Grady also wouldn't just leave his gun and walk away."

"He knew how it had to end," Dawson said quietly, his voice thick with sorrow for both Grady and Aaron.

Colt shrugged. "Maybe he needed more than a few seconds to be okay with killing his father." At Dawson's wince, Colt relented. "Sorry. I don't know what happened to Aaron's gun; he probably lost it when he got jumped. Anyhow, Aaron went for Grady's gun, and in the struggle, it went off. Killed Aaron. Grady walked home, covered in blood, and told Uncle Denny what happened. Denny took care of the body."

"Jesus," Dawson murmured. "What did they tell the cops?"

"Sheriff Rollins knew about the rogue were. He had his men out looking for it, too. So what went down could have happened to anyone."

At least no one was going to jail. That was a small comfort. "What about Knox?" Grady's older brother ran a hardware store in town, now that he couldn't hunt anymore.

"Knox is Knox," Colt replied. "He was already in danger of losing the store since he's been drinking all the profits. This isn't going to help. But you know Knox...no one can tell him anything." Dawson knew that the impatience in Colt's voice came from years of frustration, trying to help Knox get clean and being rebuffed at every attempt. "From what I heard, Knox turned his back on the whole thing."

If Knox was crawling into a bottle, he wasn't going to be any good to Grady.

"You said Uncle Denny didn't want to leave Grady. What's that *really* mean?"

"It means that for the first week after Aaron's death, Grady wouldn't eat, wouldn't talk. Uncle Denny got him to move into the second guest room at his house, and Grady didn't come out except to use the bathroom," Colt said. "He blames himself."

Dawson knew the pain of losing parents first-hand. Still, knowing that his parents had died in a plane crash was a world apart from being right there when it happened, spattered with blood, fighting for a grip on the gun. He didn't even want to imagine what Grady must be feeling.

"We take turns being home with him," Colt added quietly.

"In other words, you're afraid he'll hurt himself."

"Yeah."

Dawson closed his eyes and tried to breathe. He'd imagined his homecoming so many times, but never like this. He and Grady had finally worked things out between them, after the first three rocky years of Dawson's deployment. They'd agreed to give this new aspect of their relationship a shot once Dawson returned. For Dawson, this was more than "a shot." He meant for this thing between them to last. And now, he didn't know what to do.

Grady knew that there was no cure for a werewolf bite. Aaron would have become one of the monsters that he'd spent his life hunting. Letting him live wasn't an option.

Except it shouldn't have been his son pulling the trigger, even if Grady had been trying to take the gun away. Dawson knew that Uncle Denny had to be mourning Aaron's death, leaving him the last of the three brothers. Aaron might not have been a King by blood, but he was loved just as much all the same. But Grady...

Oh, God. Just let him make it through this okay, Dawson begged, though he'd never been overly religious. Grady was his best friend and the man he'd been in love with for four years. Whatever Dawson could do to help, he was on board. All his protective instincts came to the fore and pushed his hopes for their reunion firmly to the back of his mind.

Grady needed him as a friend right now. He certainly didn't need the complication of a relationship. So just like when he enlisted, Dawson swallowed down his feelings and resolved to do what was best for Grady. Taking care of Grady was all that mattered.

He just hoped it would be enough.

2

GRADY

GRADY KING SAT ON THE EDGE OF THE BED, STARING AT HIS HANDS. Today was supposed to be a celebration. God, he'd been looking forward to this for months.

Dawson was coming home.

Grady had been counting down the days like a kid waiting for Christmas. It had taken time and effort, but he and Dawson had reconnected over the past year, in a new and stronger way. *Or maybe I just grew up.*

They'd talked out the old hurts, discovered new interests in common, gotten to know each other in a way they couldn't have without the physical separation. That had forced them to "use their words" as Uncle Denny always chided. They emailed and connected by video when Dawson had downtime between missions.

Not only had they rekindled a rock-steady friendship, but the attraction between them survived Dawson's absence. They always had to be careful about what they said, given that the Army didn't fully welcome gay soldiers, but Grady and Dawson had known each other for so long, they could basically speak in their own code. And they had promised each other they'd give this new level of their relationship a chance once he got home.

And then *it* happened.

Grady barely acknowledged the knock at the door. Uncle Denny opened it just enough to be able to see inside. "Are you hungry?"

Grady shook his head. "Not really."

"Dawson's plane got delayed—again," Uncle Denny said. "Adds at least another hour, and that's assuming there aren't missed connections. You might as well come down for a sandwich so you don't faint from hunger before he gets here."

Grady got up and followed his uncle out of the room, grateful that Denny didn't try to keep up a conversation. He appreciated everything the older man had done for him—taking him in, making his father's final arrangements, trying to assure that he ate and slept. Grady just didn't feel much of anything *since*.

Even the excitement over Dawson's return felt muted as if he was watching someone else's reactions from a distance. Guilt, sadness, and razor-sharp self-recrimination were the only clear feelings. Grady knew he was spiraling, but he had no idea how to pull up.

"Have a seat." Denny motioned to a place at the kitchen table where a drink and a sandwich sat ready, next to a bag of Grady's favorite chips.

Nothing looked good, but Grady choked down the sandwich and managed to finish a glass of milk so he didn't seem ungrateful.

"It takes time, Grady."

He looked up and found Denny watching him with a kind expression. Grady could see the hurt in the older man's eyes and remembered that Denny had lost his brother, just as much as Grady had lost his father.

The three brothers looked so different. Grady's father had been just under six feet tall, with a compact, muscular build—a constant reminder to Aaron that he was adopted, although no one in the family ever brought it up or cared about the difference. Ethan had been a few inches taller, with a lean, runner's build—much like Dawson's. Denny was in between the other two in height and build. Ethan and Denny had the same deep-set dark eyes, a trait that ran in the King family.

Grady took more after his mother's side with dark blond hair, blue eyes, and a square jaw, but he had his father's build.

"Losing someone—it takes time. And just as soon as you think you're getting a grip, it comes back around and wallops you again. Until you realize that the hits still hurt, but they aren't as hard as they used to be. And you settle in," Denny went on, not making eye contact.

"Was it like that, when Daw's father died?"

Denny's expression grew wistful. "Worse, really. Because we know what killed your daddy, and the thing that did it is dead. But the plane crash that got Ethan and Jackie, we still don't know why it happened. Could have been what the examiners ruled, plain old bad maintenance and engine failure. But we'd tangled with a nasty coven of witches not long before, and I've always thought that it wouldn't take much magic to loosen a bolt here or there, bend a piece of metal just enough to fail."

Holy shit. I never even thought about that. "Does Daw think it was more than an accident?"

Denny shrugged. "We haven't talked about it in a long time. I imagine that the possibility has crossed his mind."

Dawson had been seventeen at the time his parents died, Grady only fifteen. Now that he knew first-hand just how fierce the loss was, Grady wondered if he had done enough back then to help Dawson through it. He didn't remember doing anything special, and he feared he might have unintentionally let Dawson down.

"You helped him a lot," Uncle Denny said as if he had read Grady's mind. "You didn't tiptoe around him or treat him any different. And whether you two were out on a hunt or just driving too fast in the Mustang, being with you cheered him up. I really think you were the reason he came through it all as well as he did. And now, he can return the favor."

Grady looked down. "We should be celebrating because he got home safely. I don't want to take that away from him."

Denny made a dismissive noise. "You aren't taking anything away. You see that cake over there? And the pile of cookies people have been dropping off all day? And the half a pig I've got in the smoker out back? We'll make sure he knows he's welcome. Nothing says 'we missed you' like a whole lot of good food."

Or "sorry for your loss," Grady thought.

For the past week, friends and distant relations had been dropping off casseroles, pies, potato salad, and enough banana pudding to last for the rest of eternity. They lingered on the porch to talk to Denny, telling him how sorry they were about Aaron's death. Grady made sure to stay out of their way. He couldn't deal with their pity, no matter how well-intentioned.

Of course, only a handful knew the real story. Everyone else had been told Aaron died in a horrific car accident and had left behind a request for a quick cremation without a funeral.

"Maybe I should go back to Dad's house. I'm not going to be good company," Grady said, although the thought made his stomach twist in disappointment. Two weeks ago, *before*, he'd been so excited about Dawson's homecoming that he had spent a whole morning figuring out what to wear to welcome him.

I managed to shave and shower today. That's more than I've done in a while.

"You're a grown-ass man, and you can do what you want," Uncle Denny replied. "I'm not going to make you stay. But...I know for a fact that Dawson is looking forward to seeing you. A lot. He won't care if you're quiet. Hell, we need to remember that he's seen things and done things over there that have changed him, too. None of us are who we were four years ago. You ever think that coming back is going to be a big adjustment for him too?"

Grady swallowed hard. "I know. And I'll stay. I just don't want to disappoint him."

"Don't think that's possible," Denny replied.

"Does he know? About what happened?" Grady felt his heart in his throat.

"If I know Dawson, he pried it out of Colt before they got out of the parking deck," Denny said with a sigh. "So I imagine he'll know enough to get the gist, anyhow."

Grady knew Dawson would have realized something had gone wrong when neither he nor Denny showed up at the airport. He just...couldn't. And even though he felt guilty for keeping Denny from going, Grady was glad for the company. The inside of his mind was a dark and dangerous place these days.

Denny set a couple of chocolate chip cookies in front of him. "Eat these. Then go for a walk and clear your head. Colt hasn't texted me yet, so they're not on their way back. You've got time."

Grady smiled his thanks. "I think I'll do that."

Denny raised an eyebrow. "Don't make me come looking for you. Dawson's going to want to see you straight off."

In other words, don't fuck this up by doing something stupid, Grady mentally translated.

"I know."

He took the cookies and headed out onto the broad wooden porch. Denny's big Rottweiler, Angel, lifted his head, eyeing Grady for a moment before he went back to sleep.

Grady paused for a moment on the top step. The view of the valley took his breath away, even though he saw it every day. The swath of forest appeared unbroken from here, though he knew roads threaded between the trees, and a handful of houses were tucked here and there among them.

He glanced down the lane to his left. He couldn't see the house where he'd grown up from here. At some point he'd need to make decisions about everything, deal with the will, the business side of dying. But not now. Maybe not for a while.

Grady ambled down the steps, deep in thought. His feet knew the way to a trail that led down toward a small lake. It had always been one of his favorite spots. He and Dawson often fished there if no pressing hunt demanded their attention. Just the two of them, usually with a six-pack of beer Dawson always managed to acquire, though they had both been underage.

Of course, Grady spent part of their time together doing little things to see if he could get Dawson's attention. Grady would strip off his shirt, or bend over from the waist as he got bait out of the bucket, giving Dawson a good show. For a long time, he felt certain Dawson was oblivious.

Grady, on the other hand, had been painfully aware of Dawson's every move.

He found a place on a rise overlooking the lake where he could sit with his back to a tree and look out over the water, watching it sparkle in the sun.

When they were growing up, that two-year difference in age mattered a lot. Dawson and Knox hung out with the older teens, off doing almost-adult stuff while Grady remained relegated to the group of younger cousins. Even then, he'd been drawn to Dawson, who barely noticed him.

At first it had been hero worship. Dawson and the older boys challenged each other to marksmanship contests, raced their cars on back roads, and swapped stories about their hunts, which tended to grow with the telling. Grady dreamed of the day when he'd be old enough to do exciting stuff like that, and be accepted by the "big kids."

Then Grady hit puberty, and he started noticing Dawson for a whole different set of reasons, like his muscular arms, strong back, and perfect ass. It had scared Grady at first because he knew exactly what his mother thought about someone who got involved with their cousin, even though he and Dawson weren't related by blood. That detail wouldn't have mattered to her. *Dirty, disgusting, wrong.*

But Camille was gone, and she wasn't coming back. She hadn't cared enough to stick around for her two sons, so Grady wasn't inclined to worry overmuch about what she might make of his secret fantasies.

Dawson, on the other hand, was an entirely different matter. Grady did his best not to be caught ogling his older cousin. He knew Dawson was gay—Dawson hadn't made a secret of it, although he also didn't go out of his way to broadcast the fact. Grady had just begun to figure his own issues out. So it wasn't like Dawson would hate him or reject him for the very idea.

Grady used to worry that perhaps Dawson agreed with Camille

about the whole "cousins" thing. Just because it wasn't technically true for them didn't mean Dawson would accept a relationship being okay, any more than Grady's mother would have. Or worse, what if he could never get over seeing Grady as just one of the kids who horsed around and made too much noise at picnics and holidays?

When Grady turned fifteen, and he and Dawson began to hunt together, Grady discovered spending time with his crush was equal parts torture and bliss. On those long drives and stakeouts, he had Dawson's undivided attention. He tried to be funny, to show that he wasn't a kid anymore. Sometimes, he even looked up odd trivia to throw out in conversation.

Dawson humored him, never made fun or acted condescending. After a year, Grady got comfortable enough that he and Dawson fell into a natural rhythm. Those were his best memories, Grady recalled. They'd go into a hunt with research and plans and end up improvising, then make it out by the skin of their teeth, running for their lives.

God, Dawson was even more attractive like that, face streaked with dirt and sweat, breathing hard from the run, skin flushed from the adrenaline. Grady always had to adjust himself to avoid Dawson noticing how hard he'd gotten at the sight.

Sometimes, when Grady was in school, Dawson and Colt hunted together. At first, he didn't think anything of it, since the two had been friends for a long time. But the longer it went on, the more suspicious Grady became.

Dawson and Colt never acted like boyfriends. But now and again, Grady caught a tone of voice or a shared look that didn't seem quite right. The two often came up with a reason to make hunts into overnight trips. Still, Grady hadn't figured it out until the two of them went out to the barn one evening to "clean the guns."

They'd come back with rumpled hair, badly buttoned shirts, and expressions that could only be described as "fucked out." Uncle Denny took them aside for a stern word. Grady went home and hid in his room for the rest of the day, too upset to be civil.

After that, Dawson and Colt quit hunting together for a while.

Grady started hunting with Dawson more often. At night, alone in his bed, Grady pictured Dawson's toned body next to him, imagined being able to touch all that beautiful skin and lean muscle, kiss those full lips. He'd pretend it was Dawson's strong hand and calloused palm on his cock instead of his own, remembered the smell of his shampoo, and it always made Grady come embarrassingly fast. Then he'd hide the evidence, manage a smile, and meet up with Dawson again for another day of blissful frustration.

They had a good time, and occasionally Grady caught a furtive glance in his direction, making him wonder if Dawson was finally, *finally* beginning to notice him.

Until Dawson started to make a habit of inventing reasons to make "supply runs" to Asheville every few weeks, far more often than anyone needed to go before. Usually the day after he and Grady had been on a hunt. He didn't get back until the wee hours of the morning from those runs, and Grady couldn't overlook that Dawson sure dressed well to go pick up ammo.

Which meant he was really going out to get laid.

When Grady figured that out, he had just turned seventeen. He swiped a bottle of whiskey from his dad's stash and went to the barn to get drunk, sick with jealousy. When his father found him, Grady lied and said he'd been angry about getting dumped by a girl at school. He didn't talk to Dawson for a week.

After that, Grady had decided to forget his crush on Dawson. He started working out beyond his usual training for the hunt. Whenever he wasn't in school or hunting, he lifted weights and ran. It didn't take long to see his body change, fill out, no longer a scrawny kid.

One of his gamer friends from high school invited him over for an all-night video game marathon and made advances. Grady went along with it, figuring that maybe if he wasn't completely inexperienced, it would make a difference, and he could win Dawson's attention. He wore those hickeys like a badge of honor, making sure he was marked somewhere visible. Dawson clearly noticed, but didn't say anything.

He and Dawson still hunted together, more often than ever. Most of the time, they clicked. They were good together, and it just made

Grady's heart ache for what he couldn't have. Dawson remained his best friend, and if things went south on a hunt, the older man could be a fierce protector. But never anything more.

And now, when he and Dawson were—*finally*—going to be on the same page, Grady was an emotional mess. *And isn't that just my luck?*

What would Dawson think, when he heard about Aaron's death? Would he blame Grady? Be disappointed that Grady hadn't been faster to take out the werewolf? Could he ever trust Grady to have his back on a hunt again?

If Dawson couldn't trust him, then exploring their attraction, trying to start a relationship would never work. That thought hurt enough to bring tears to his eyes.

Maybe he's just planning to let you down easy, in person. You got your own father killed on a hunt. Why would anyone trust you as any kind of partner, ever again? a traitorous voice whispered in the back of Grady's mind.

After all, Grady blamed himself. Why wouldn't anyone else? He'd replayed those frantic seconds over and over, awake and in his nightmares.

———

ONE WEEK AGO

His dad had been in front, with Grady watching the rear. They'd lost the creature's tracks but felt certain they knew where it would head. The dark, quiet forest offered too many places to hide.

The werewolf seemed to come out of nowhere ahead of them, so close to Aaron that he'd had to take a step back to raise his gun. The were's teeth sank into Aaron's shoulder, and with his dad between him and the werewolf, Grady couldn't get off a clean shot.

"Shoot!" Aaron ordered.

Grady couldn't.

The werewolf tossed Aaron to the side and rushed Grady. Grady's finger squeezed the trigger and his aim held true. The silver bullet hit the creature center mass, right in the heart. It fell to its knees with a roar, then collapsed, dead.

Grady ran to help his father, hoping that he'd been wrong about the bite, knowing that he wasn't. Aaron had lost a lot of blood. The werewolf's fangs punctured deep, and the other teeth tore flesh. If it had been any other creature, Aaron might have lost his arm. But they both knew what a werewolf's bite meant.

"We could have been wrong," Grady said, his tone pleading, his mouth dry. "Maybe it was a shifter."

Aaron glanced up at the sky, where the full moon shone brightly through the trees. "He's only ever been out when the moon is full. No kills any other time. That's not a shifter." Pain made his voice hitch, and he sounded resigned.

"There's got to be something—"

"Do it." Aaron met his eyes, pleading with him to understand.

"I can't."

"Then leave me the gun and go. Denny will take care of everything."

"Dad, no. There has to be another way."

Aaron surged up, moving faster than Grady thought possible given the wound, going for his gun. Grady tightened his grip as years of training kicked in. Aaron tried to pry his fingers loose.

The gun went off. Grady froze, not sure which of them had been shot. Then he saw blood blooming from Aaron's chest, felt his father stagger and caught him, slowly lowering the dying man to the ground. Aaron was gone, leaving Grady alone in the forest with two corpses, covered in their blood.

———

PRESENT DAY

Footsteps crunched on sticks and dry leaves, intentionally announcing the newcomer's arrival, since hunters knew how to move silently. Grady knew he hadn't been gone long enough for Dawson to arrive.

"I thought I might find you out here," Uncle Denny said. "It's a pretty place to sort your thoughts. Probably one of my favorites on the whole mountain."

"I wasn't going to run away. Or do anything stupid."

"Didn't think you were."

They were both lying, and they both knew it.

"Colt texted. They're on their way from Asheville."

Grady swallowed hard. He wanted to bolt and keep on running. Or maybe plunge into the lake and never come up.

Denny had made it clear, over and over again, that he didn't blame Grady for Aaron's death. But how could he not? Grady sure blamed himself. If he'd just been faster, if he'd gone first, if they had gone a different trail...

"I'll say it as many times as you need to hear it—it's not your fault. I don't blame you. And I'm sure your dad didn't blame you. Aaron knew what would happen from that bite. He wouldn't judge you." Denny paused. "And Dawson won't either."

"You don't know that for sure." Grady's voice sounded small and uncertain.

"I know Dawson. And so do you." Denny's voice, firm but kind, made Grady raise his hopes.

"Okay." Grady took a deep breath and let it out. He trusted Dawson. Loved him. They'd already worked out a lot of the old issues on those late-night video calls. This was a fresh start. He just had to believe a little longer.

"How about coming back up to the house, help me with the barbecue?" Denny asked, keeping his tone light. "By the time we finish with that, Colt and Dawson should be here."

They walked back in companionable silence. Grady knew he was a worry to his uncle, who ought to be able to grieve his own loss without dealing with Grady's shit.

"I'm glad you moved in," Denny said, with that weird perfect timing of his. "The house was too quiet with Dawson gone, and lately, I'm glad not to be alone with my thoughts."

You and me both. Grady didn't remember the immediate aftermath of that night clearly, except that Denny coaxed the details of the hunt from him, then got Colt to stay with Grady while Denny went out. Grady didn't know what he might have done without Denny, and he didn't want to imagine the possibilities.

"There's plenty of room, even with Dawson back," Denny went on. "I kinda like the idea of having the two of you underfoot again. Like old times."

Right. Moody, hungry, and overflowing with unresolved sexual tension. "That'll be nice."

Denny turned and made eye contact for the first time. "I fully believe you two will figure everything out. Just...take things one step at a time. You'll get where you need to be."

Grady had always suspected that Denny knew more than he let on about the mess between him and Dawson. Maybe he hadn't been as stealthy as he thought he was back in the day. And maybe it hadn't been all his imagination that Dawson noticed and wanted Grady just as much. His uncle was always careful not to confirm that suspicion, and Grady didn't know exactly how to feel about that.

If his mother had suspected, her head would have exploded. She'd have probably yanked him off the mountain and dragged him with her, away from "bad influences." And if Denny actively opposed him and Dawson being anything more than friends, he figured Denny wouldn't have invited him to move in. Denny knew how to mind his own business, but that didn't keep him from nudging people one way or another when he thought it necessary.

They got back to the house, and Grady felt butterflies in his stomach. He hadn't been out of his room this much since *it* happened, or talked as much. He certainly didn't feel like his old self. *And maybe I never will.* A stew of conflicting emotions brewed inside him, fraying raw nerves.

Denny gave him one easy task after another that kept Grady busy. Helping with the pig roast was something Grady and the other kids in the family had done from the time they were old enough to be judged trustworthy around the huge, very hot smoker. Denny was the family pitmaster, and over the years he had done the honors for weddings, graduations, anniversaries, and birthday bashes.

Grady stopped and took a deep breath, inhaling the scent of smoke, roasting meat, and the cherry wood used for the fire. With his eyes closed, enveloped by that familiar aroma, Grady could pretend, just for a moment, that nothing had changed.

The crunch of tires on the gravel driveway shattered the illusion, and Grady tensed. Moments later, he heard voices, and then footsteps coming around back to the smoker.

Angel came tearing around the house, barking like a maniac, and ran toward the two newcomers, wagging hard.

Grady looked up, and for a second he almost didn't recognize the man with Colt. The video calls they'd traded over the years didn't capture the changes. A regulation buzzcut heightened the man's haggard appearance, with more than a day's worth of scruff and worried eyes.

Grady froze, heart thudding. "Dawson?"

3

DAWSON

Dawson didn't think; he acted. He crossed the last few feet in long strides and pulled Grady into a bone-crushing hug. For a second, Grady stiffened, and then he leaned in, clutching Dawson like a drowning man.

"Gray," he managed, his throat tight, falling into using the old nickname.

"Welcome home, Daw," Grady replied in a thick voice.

A lifetime of vigilance trained Dawson to take in details in a glance. In those few seconds before he grabbed Grady, what Dawson saw scared him. Grady's eyes were haunted, smudged with dark circles. Only a week had passed since Aaron's death, but Grady looked gaunt like he'd dropped weight fast.

Still, this was Grady, his "Gray," real and alive, and hugging him back. Dawson took in the smell of sweat and soap and shaving cream that he associated with Grady. For a few seconds longer, he clung to the contact, aware that Grady was hugging back just as fiercely. Then he stepped away, leaving a hand on Grady's shoulder.

"I probably stink," Dawson said, trying to lighten the mood. "Haven't had a shower since I left the base, which was a while ago."

"No different from all the times you came home ripe from a

hunt," Denny said. Dawson squeezed Grady's shoulder and then stepped into his uncle's embrace.

"Glad you're back in one piece, boy," Denny murmured, voice shaky.

Dawson didn't trust his voice for a moment, overcome by emotion. "It's good to be home," he managed.

"Why don't you go clean up?" Denny said. "Drop your bag in your old room; everything's ready for you. The pig'll be done shortly." He looked to Colt. "Thanks for picking him up. Can you stay for dinner?"

Colt shook his head. "Thanks, but I promised to be somewhere tonight. In fact, I'd better run. Take it easy, y'all." With that, he sprinted back to his truck and roared off.

Dawson chuckled. "He's got a hot date. I'm lucky he didn't just slow down and push me out when we got to the driveway."

"Go," Denny told him. "I don't want to have to sit downwind from you."

Dawson hitched his duffel bag higher on his shoulder, gave one more worried glance in Grady's direction, and then headed inside, glad for the few minutes the shower provided to pull himself together.

Just being home brought so many emotions to the surface. He'd missed everything about the mountain. Dawson still wasn't sure whether his stint in the Army had been a necessary move or a colossal mistake. The verdict was still out. But he'd dreamed of this day for so long—not just for Grady, but because of so many things.

Especially Grady.

God, it felt so good to hug him tight. Taking in Grady's scent, hearing his voice went right to Dawson's cock, and he suspected, from the way Grady had shifted, that it might have had the same effect on the other man as well.

Dawson stripped out of his fatigues, leaving them in a pile he'd worry about on laundry day. He ran the shower as hot as he could stand it and chuckled when he found a bar of Irish Spring waiting for him, a smell he associated with home.

For several moments he reveled in the hot water, good pressure, and privacy. He lathered up his short hair, resolving to grow it out now that he could. As he washed the rest of his body, his fingers traced old scars. Some were from hunting. The bullet wound over his ribs, and the ugly gash left by shrapnel were new, and Dawson had been lucky to survive them.

Dawson shut down the bad memories. There would be time enough for that later. Now, he had other concerns. Like how to help Grady.

He and Grady had managed a video call just two weeks ago, giddy over his upcoming return. During the four years Dawson was gone, they had both changed—Dawson from the stress of a war zone, and Grady from maturing from teen to man. He'd thought how handsome Grady had become as his body filled out, and his face lost some of its boyishness.

Dawson hadn't been prepared for the stark change the last week had brought. Grady had the look of a man fresh from the front lines who had seen horrors beyond words. And maybe, Dawson thought, that comparison wasn't far off. What happened with Grady and Aaron was just as traumatic as the heat of battle, only without a cast of thousands.

And then there was the secret Dawson had been carrying, one he couldn't even trust to Denny. A week ago—which would have been just before Aaron died—Dawson had dreamed of a Black Shuck, a monstrous black dog, much like the hellhounds that gave Cunanoon Mountain its name. But dreaming of a Shuck was a death omen. The dream hadn't made sense until Colt's story on the way back from the airport. Dawson had only dreamed of a Shuck a few other times. One dream had come right before his unit had been ambushed, and they'd all nearly died. And then another just two days ago, the night before he left base.

Now that he knew what had happened to Aaron, Dawson couldn't shake the fear that the latest omen was meant for Grady. But he'd always heard that to speak of an omen was to make it come true, and it wasn't exactly something he could research on his heavily-monitored Army internet connection. Now that he was home, did he dare ask Denny about it? Or did he need to remain silent about the shuck to protect Grady?

Even if he couldn't tell anyone else about the omen, that wouldn't stop Dawson from protecting Grady with his life. But it was yet another reason to put the brakes on moving too fast into a new level to their relationship. Getting lost in emotion could distract Dawson, and he needed to keep a clear head if he wanted to save Grady.

He shaved, then shut off the water before it cooled and reached for a towel, trying to remember what they'd been told about PTSD in the Army's mental health updates. The idea hadn't been new to Dawson; he'd seen older hunters with the telltale signs, and he had his own issues. He wouldn't be surprised, given what happened, if Grady was struggling with some level of PTSD. Dawson also knew that sort of thing didn't magically go away. It would take time, patience, and focus for Grady to heal. Dawson intended to be right there with him every step of the way.

But how to ease back into being together without rushing Grady or adding the tricky emotions of a new relationship to already-raw nerves, while keeping him safe? That left Dawson at a loss.

If I do what's best for him, we'll get the chance to do what's right for us, he told himself. That didn't stop him from chafing at the delay, after being far away for far too long.

Then again, maybe it shouldn't be a surprise that moving to a new phase in their relationship would come on the heels of a near-death experience. That had been true from the beginning, as Dawson well remembered.

———

Four Years Ago

He and Grady searched for three missing deer hunters. Dawson felt certain a vengeful spirit was to blame. At nineteen and seventeen, Dawson and Grady were already seasoned hunters, and angry spirits were a relatively straightforward problem to solve. Aaron and Denny were off hunting a Shuck, several counties away. Sheriff Rollins and his wolf-shifter pack of deputies had their hands full with an over-turned tractor-trailer blocking the main road through the valley. That left Grady and Dawson to look into the problem since Colt was flat on his ass with strep throat.

"They're saying it might snow," Grady said as they parked the Mustang in the lot at the bottom of the trail. Both men slipped hand-guns into the backs of their waistbands, and Ka-bars into the sheaths on their belts. Dawson had more weapons in the pack, just in case.

"Last I saw, it's not supposed to roll in until morning," Dawson replied. "We'll be long gone and back home warming up by the fire." He pulled a duffel bag full of weapons and supplies from the trunk. "The guys who went missing were just scouting for deer. It's only two days until buck season opens, and these hills will be crawling with hunters in camo and orange vests. If we don't stop the ghost, there'll be more missing hunters—and dead ones."

Dawson knew that once they got farther up the mountain their phones would lose signal. He still threw their phones in the pack, just in case. They headed up the trail, shoulder to shoulder, alert for trouble.

"Rollins and his deputies were out here, looking for the hunters. They didn't find anything—and they're shifters," Grady reminded him. The bright sun and brisk air made for a good day to be outside, and Dawson was looking forward to the chili simmering in the slow cooker back home for dinner.

"Shifters rely too much on their noses," Dawson said. "Can't smell a ghost."

This area was a likely spot for a vengeful spirit. Kit Johnson and his hunting partner had gone looking for deer on this slope the previous year. They'd gotten to a remote section, then argued. The reports Dawson had read suggested alcohol and jealousy were involved. Johnson's partner shot him dead and left the body where it fell. In his haste to leave the scene, the killer ran his car off the road and died. No one found Johnson for several weeks. By then, scavengers had made short work of his body and carried off several bones, which were never found.

All three of this year's missing hunters had left word that they were heading into that same remote area.

"If we don't have Johnson's bones, how are we going to banish his ghost?" Grady asked.

Dawson patted the pack he carried. "Kit's wife gave me some things that belonged to him. A hat, a hunting jacket, and his favorite baseball card. If we do the ritual right, we should be able to trap his ghost in the possessions and then salt and burn them to set him free."

Grady raised an eyebrow. "You ever do this before?"

Dawson grinned. "Not exactly like this, no. But Denny read over the ritual and said it'll work."

"What are we waiting for then?" Grady gave a mischievous smile. "The sooner we light this ghost up, the sooner we get home to eat Uncle Denny's chili and cornbread." He took off, getting ahead of Dawson on the trail. "C'mon, slow butt!"

Dawson didn't miss the sway of Grady's hips or the way his jeans showed off his firm ass and muscular thighs. He knew Grady intended him to notice. Grady's efforts were far more successful than his younger cousin realized.

Grady King had grown up almost overnight, from a skinny kid to a very attractive young man. At seventeen, Grady seemed to think he knew what he wanted—and what he wanted was Dawson.

Dawson really hadn't noticed Grady that way until a few months before. He'd had that uncomfortable revelation one day when he found himself paying far too much attention to Grady's broad shoulders and strong back when the two of them had been chopping firewood. All of a sudden, odd comments and actions he'd dismissed assembled to provide a whole new perspective.

Grady had been flirting with him, trying hard to get his attention. The realization left Dawson poleaxed, and then uneasy, because while he had dismissed Grady as a kid before, he sure as hell wasn't a kid any longer. Dawson's reaction made it very clear his body was completely on board, even if his better judgment pointed out all the ways that acting on his attraction would be a really bad idea. Either way, he couldn't go back to the way things were.

"If I beat you to the top, your ass is grass!" Grady called, egging Dawson on. No matter what might be changing between them, the banter came naturally, like always. Dawson enjoyed spending time with Grady, hunting or not. He admired Grady's sass and determination. Being with Grady even made chores fun.

Dawson checked his compass, then glanced at the paper map he'd brought, expecting poor phone reception. He had marked the coordinates of the off-the-beaten-trail location where the hunters had gone missing and Johnson's remains had been found. "This is where we leave the trail," he called out to Grady. "Better let me go first—I'm the one with the map."

"Suits me," Grady replied, "I'm just enjoying the walk and the view." Dawson moved up, and Grady fell in a few steps behind him.

Dawson's cheeks heated. Grady's tone had been conversational, nothing he could be called out on. But Dawson knew the intent had been anything but innocent. Even worse, his cock got the message loud and clear, chubbing up uncomfortably.

Both men knew their way around the woods. Growing up on the mountain, learning outdoor skills went hand-in-hand with training to hunt monsters. Yet for all the time they had hiked these hills, Dawson couldn't recall ever venturing into this area. It certainly wasn't easy to get to, and he didn't envy the sportsmen trying to drag a prize buck all the way back to the parking lot.

Then again, deer hunters were always looking for a less known corner of the woods to call their own.

"This should be the spot," Dawson said when they reached the place where Kit Johnson's body had been found. "Watch my back while I lay out the ritual, and then we can head home for that chili." The air had grown steadily colder as they hiked, and steel-gray clouds rolled in. He wondered if the forecast had gotten it wrong, and hoped they could get down off the mountain before the bad weather hit.

Dawson set down the duffel bag and pulled out what he needed, as well as two shotguns. He loaded them with shells that held a mixture of rock salt and iron pellets, both of which worked to dispel ghosts. That wouldn't banish Johnson's spirit, but it would hold him off if he attacked. He passed one of the shotguns to Grady and kept the other close.

He laid out the hat, jacket, and baseball card on the ground and stepped back. "Kit Johnson," he called into the wind. "I brought your things. It's time for you to move on."

The wind picked up and grew even colder until both men could see their breath. A shimmer in the air served as the only warning before a tall, long-limbed creature appeared out of nowhere, just a few feet from Dawson. The monster's skin stretched taut over its visible skeleton, and blackened lips pulled back to reveal sharpened yellow teeth.

"Shit—Johnson's ghost turned wendigo!" Dawson barely had time to warn Grady before the monster came at him. He blasted it with the shotgun, and it vanished, then reappeared on the other side. An all-too-solid arm clotheslined Dawson before he could get in another shot, sending him flying. He hit a tree hard and came down on his left leg with an audible crunch. Pain seared through Dawson, and he knew he'd broken a bone.

"Hey, ugly!" Grady shouted, trying to draw the creature's attention. He fired a silver bullet from his handgun, the proper way to get rid of a wendigo. But the creature dodged, and the bullet missed its heart. Dawson crawled for the duffel, going for the flare gun he had brought.

Before Grady could react, the monster was on him, slashing sharp claws across his chest and going for the kill with its long fangs. Grady brought the handgun up and pumped his last bullet into the creature's heart, just as Dawson dragged himself into position to fire a flare and set the hat, card, and jacket on fire. The wendigo reared, let out a blood-curdling scream, and crumbled into a shower of ash and cinders.

"What...the hell...was that?" Grady managed between clenched teeth.

"We'll figure it out once you stop bleeding." Pain shot through Dawson as he crawled closer, dragging the duffel with him. He felt the bones in his leg move like they were grinding, and the chill that settled in his limb hinted he was going into shock. Dawson bit his lip hard. He caught his breath when he registered the damage the creature's claws had done to Grady. Four deep gashes ripped through Grady's coat and shirt, tearing into the skin below. Blood soaked the tattered clothing.

Dawson tried to keep his broken leg straight as he tore off a piece of Grady's ruined shirt to use as a compress. Stopping the bleeding only solved part of the problem. Wendigo claws carried infection, and that kind of thing could go bad fast. Little jabs of lightning raced through his leg and stabbed at his hip while he worked.

"Maybe there's a reason no one came up here," Dawson said, trying to keep Grady centered as he stanched the flow of blood. At the same time, he forced himself to stay alert and keep the shock at bay.

"Not the usual wendigo, huh?" Dawson said, trying to keep himself conscious and distract Grady. "I've got a theory about that."

"Wendigos usually keep to the far north, but I guess one made its way down here," Dawson continued, hoping Grady stayed focused on his voice. "They're a type of vengeful spirit that usually possesses a living human. But maybe its host eventually died, and maybe over time, the wendigo spirit faded. Then Johnson got killed, and his ghost was too angry to move on. If they somehow teamed up—or the wendigo was able to take control of Johnson's ghost, then it could manifest with more power. And be dangerous again."

Grady just groaned. The cuts had to hurt like fuck, and Dawson gritted his teeth against the lightning dancing in his leg. He knew that even if he could somehow splint the broken limb, they'd never make it back to the car, not with the steepness of the slope and the distance.

A bitter wind swept past them as flakes of snow began to fall, thick and fast.

"Shit."

"How bad is it?" Grady's weak voice drew Dawson's attention to how pale his cousin had grown.

"I need to get us to shelter, something defensible, and then I've got to close up those gashes," Dawson replied, skirting the question. Focusing on action kept his own growing panic at bay. "I'll do my best to make the scars pretty, but there's no guarantee. You can always blame them on pirates."

"Car's too far away."

"Yeah. But Colt knows where we are. He'll call Aaron and Denny when we miss our check-in. They'll find us." Except that Aaron and Denny weren't close—the hunt they'd gone on was some distance away. Help wouldn't be coming anytime soon.

Dawson pulled himself up on his good knee to look around. The broken bone shifted and felt surreal. He welcomed the pain; if it stopped hurting shock was taking hold. Then they'd be really screwed.

He spotted a rocky outcropping with enough of an overhang to form a shallow cave. "I think I just found us a room for the night."

Grady forced himself up with a cry and reached out to help Dawson onto his good leg. "This is the weirdest three-legged race ever," he grated, face drawn with agony. Dawson bit back a moan as his leg jostled, hanging loose like a noodle. He muttered a continuous stream of curses under his breath as Grady half-carried, half-dragged him.

With considerable effort, they made it to the outcropping and collapsed, exhausted. On closer inspection, "cave" overstated the shallow depression, but it was recessed enough to blunt the wind and keep the snow off them.

Grady's quick, shallow breathing, and his pallor told Dawson the bleeding had started up again. Grady closed his eyes and drifted off.

Somehow, Dawson needed to gather sticks so he could set a fire at the mouth of their shelter. They'd need the warmth, and it would serve to keep predators away and provide a beacon for Aaron and Denny.

It took three trips to drag a couple of bundles of sticks, his duffel, and a fallen, half-rotted branch substantial enough to last for a while. Dawson sweated despite the dropping temperatures, and his leg throbbed in time with his heart. He rustled through the duffel, pulling out matches and a can of Sterno. Minutes later, a fire burned between them and the darkness. The canned heat would keep a paltry flame lit for a few hours, providing little warmth. He worried that the wood wasn't going to be enough for the night.

It hit Dawson that the odds were good that they could die before someone found them. Would their ghosts rise to be the new haunts of this place?

"Hey, how're you holding up?" he asked Grady, whose uncharacteristic silence scared him.

"Been better. You?"

"Still on the right side of the dirt."

A little more rummaging, and Dawson found the small field medic kit and the flask of whiskey he'd thrown in on a whim. He also pulled out a shiny "space blanket" emergency wrap to keep them warm once he finished treating Grady's wounds.

"Drink this," he said, knowing that cleaning and closing the wounds was going to hurt like hell, but it was the only way to keep Grady from losing more blood. Dawson held the flask so Grady could manage a couple of swallows, gasping as the potent liquor burned down his throat.

"I've got antibiotic cream, but no painkillers," he told Grady. "So the whiskey is going to have to do."

"I'm cold," Grady murmured.

That could mean blood loss, shock, or hypothermia, none of them good. The liquor would help ease the pain but created a risk of losing body heat faster.

"You're in luck," Dawson replied, keeping his voice light although his stomach knotted. "We've got Steri-Strips, so I don't have to practice my sewing on you. Stay with me. I'll make this as quick as I can."

Grady chewed on his lip as Dawson made his best attempt at sterilizing the cuts and closing the gashes, then taped gauze from the kit over the wounds. He pulled Grady's shirt and ruined jacket closed, and reached for the silver blanket.

"I've got a couple of protein bars and some bottled water," he offered as he bundled them together. "You should eat something."

"Not hungry."

"Doesn't matter." Dawson managed to get Grady to eat most of one bar and choke down half a bottle of water. He finished his own rations quickly and then sidled closer to Grady and pulled the blanket around them.

"We'll stay warmer together," he said, acutely aware that they were pressed together from hip to knee, and shoulder against shoulder.

"Not exactly how I pictured spending the night with you," Grady slurred, pain and whiskey taking their toll.

He's pictured us spending the night together? Dawson thought with a start. Then again, ever since that day chopping wood, Grady had starred in most of Dawson's more explicit dreams, as well as his morning shower jerk-offs. "Spending the night together" had been on Dawson's mind, although sleep hadn't factored into those fantasies.

Grady fell asleep quickly, leaving Dawson on watch—and alone with his thoughts. He was acutely aware of the warmth of Grady's body next to his, and the rhythm of his breathing. Dawson laid a hand on Grady's forehead, worried that he might be feverish from the filth on the wendigo's claws. Dawson could only hope that Colt noticed they hadn't returned and called in the cavalry. They had enough ammunition to hold off the bobcats and wolves for another night, but if Grady's injuries didn't kill him, the predators and the cold would get them both before long.

Dawson had to stay awake. If he kept his mind busy, that would help. He could prod his leg for another jolt of pain, anything that would work. If he nodded off, there'd be no future of any kind for Grady and him.

He kept coming back to Grady's flirting, and his own reaction. He cared about Grady, felt protective toward him. When had it become something more? A memory of Grady showing up wearing a fresh hickey like a badge of honor still brought an uncomfortable surge of...jealousy? Then there'd been the time Grady stopped speaking to him after he and Colt forgot to be discreet.

Oh.

Dawson closed his eyes and let his head rest against the stone for a moment. Another stab of pain in his leg assured him that he was in no danger of falling asleep on watch.

So he and Grady had been dancing around each other for a while —longer than he'd let himself realize. He couldn't deny the attraction he felt, and something suspiciously akin to love.

But Grady was only seventeen, and other than the hickey-sucking gamer guy, Dawson didn't think Grady'd had any real boyfriends. Could his feelings for Dawson be more than a crush? How could they be, when Grady barely had a chance to do any dating, let alone figure out what being gay—or bi—meant to him.

Dawson hadn't dated anyone for very long, but he'd had his share of encounters behind the bars he frequented in Asheville. Now that he thought about it, he'd always felt desperate to make an Asheville run after he'd been in close quarters with Grady, and he didn't need a shrink to point out to him that his hookups tended to bear a resemblance to the man next to him.

At the same time, Dawson knew, deep in his heart, that if he ever did start something with Grady, it wouldn't be a hookup or a fling. If they started this, Dawson wanted forever. And he knew that was too much to ask.

What if he changes his mind? What if he discovers that he actually agrees with his crazy mother? What if he realizes that I'm not really what he wants, after all?

Then Grady would leave, and Dawson would let him go. And it would rip him to shreds.

I can't give him what he thinks he wants. At least, not now. Maybe later, after he's had a chance to figure out his own mind. But God, I don't think I can hold him off forever. I'm not that strong.

The lightning chased itself up and down Dawson's leg, his mind whirled, and he fought to stay conscious.

Aaron and Denny found them just after dawn. Dawson stuck close to Grady during the long trip to the hospital. He didn't even remember what story they'd made up to satisfy the doctor. By the time they'd set his leg, and Grady's fever broke, Dawson had a plan.

As soon as his leg healed, Dawson enlisted, asking to ship out as soon as possible. Three months later, he was gone.

———

PRESENT DAY

"Did you drown in there?" Uncle Denny's voice carried through the door. Dawson realized he'd completely lost track of time.

"No, sorry. Just spacey from the jet lag," he covered. "I'll be right down."

"We're already carrying in the meat, so if it's cold, that's your loss." Denny's footsteps retreated, and Dawson pinched the bridge of his nose, staving off a headache.

He'd had to distance himself once before, for Grady's sake. Leaving had nearly killed Dawson, but the four-year separation made him all the more certain of where his heart lay. But now, Grady needed time to heal, and Dawson had to figure out the meaning of the death omen to keep Grady safe.

Which meant Dawson had to pull back, at least a bit, postpone the kind of reunion that heated his dreams and fantasies for months, to protect Grady. This time, he wasn't going anywhere. He'd be right beside Grady until the time was right.

Dawson only hoped that Grady would see it that way.

4

GRADY

GRADY WATCHED DAWSON HEAD INTO THE HOUSE AND COULDN'T RESIST letting his gaze fall to an ass that had, impossibly, gotten even firmer than before. Their video calls really hadn't done justice to the changes military training had made to Dawson's shoulders and arms. Grady loved every second of having those strong arms wrapped around him, holding him like they would never let him go.

Even the way Dawson moved looked different. He'd always been graceful; now his movements reminded Grady of a big cat stalking its prey.

"Let's get the meat out of the smoker," Uncle Denny said, jarring Grady out of his thoughts. Denny's slight smile told Grady that his uncle had noticed.

"Uh, yeah. Sure." The sudden rush of emotions left Grady tongue-tied.

"He'll be back before you know it," Denny said, heading off toward the big black metal cylinder in the backyard. Grady glanced at the upstairs window he knew was Dawson's room, then sighed and followed.

Denny rolled back the lid on the big smoker, and the smell

managed to make Grady's stomach growl, despite the way his appetite had failed him recently.

"I mixed up a big batch of that sauce you boys like." Denny pulled on protective gloves and grabbed a knife and tongs. He jerked his head toward a large platter that lay on a nearby table, and Grady ran to get it. Denny proceeded to pile the plate high with meat from the grill.

"Go ahead and take that into the kitchen. Bring back the other plate that's in there," Denny directed. Grady walked carefully, not taking any chances with his precious burden. Throwing a "pig pickin'" was the hallmark of a real celebration in these parts. Dawson deserved that.

He couldn't quite believe the four years were already over. At one time, Grady had been certain it would never end.

———

Four Years Earlier

"Is it true?" Grady caught up with Dawson in the yard and grabbed his arm, forcing Dawson to turn to face him. "You enlisted? You're shipping out? Did you intend to tell me sometime in the next couple of days, or was I going to find out after you were gone?"

Even as angry and hurt as Grady was, he didn't miss the way Dawson winced at his tone. He saw the guilt in the other man's eyes.

"I don't want to fight with you, Gray. And yes, I was going to tell you tomorrow."

"Oh, wow. That way we could have one whole day together before you leave for four fuckin' years."

"Gray—"

"Why?" Grady demanded. "You never said a word about going into the Army all these years. Kings don't have to leave the mountain to fight a war. We've got our own right here. So why'd you do it, Daw?"

Dawson held himself as if he expected Grady to take a swing at him, and truth be told, Grady struggled to keep from doing just that. "It'll be better for both of us if I leave for a while," he said quietly.

Grady had felt his heart shatter at those words, confirming what he feared. "You're leaving because of me."

"No!" Dawson didn't meet Grady's gaze. "Not the way you think."

"Oh, so you know what I'm thinking? Please, explain it to me, because I don't want to misunderstand." Grady couldn't keep his pain and the feeling of betrayal out of his voice.

There was no way Dawson could know how Grady felt about him, was there? No, Grady had always been careful. Sure, he'd done his share of watching. But he'd always downplayed any time Dawson might have noticed with a joke, turning it back on his cousin, laughing it off.

Except, Grady didn't remember everything about that night he and Dawson spent up on the mountain after the ghost-wendigo nearly finished them both. He'd been in pain, and the whiskey on an empty stomach had gone right to his head, like it was supposed to. Then he went to sleep.

Did something happen when he was too drunk and pain-fogged to remember? Oh God, did he say something—do something—that gave away his secret? Grady had nursed hopes that, in time, Dawson could come to see him differently, that his long-time crush could turn into something real if he was just patient.

But what if Dawson *did* know, and didn't feel the same way? Maybe he still thought Grady was a kid, or not experienced enough, or maybe he "just wasn't into him like that." And then Grady had done something—*must* have done something—and Dawson was upset enough about it to leave.

Leave him, leave the family, leave the mountain.

Now that Grady thought about it, things had been different after that hunt. Dawson had pulled back. He seemed more distant—not unfriendly, just preoccupied. For a while, recovering from their injuries ruled out hunting. After that, they'd only hunted once or twice together, easy jobs, nothing that meant they had to spend a lot of time with each other. How had Grady not realized that Dawson was really saying goodbye?

"Gray, hear me out." Dawson's voice held a pleading note. Grady was too hurt and angry to care.

"I guess I'm just lucky you didn't leave me a note. I thought I was your best friend!" *And I wanted to be so much more. I love you, goddammit. Please, please don't hate me for it.*

"You *are* my best friend," Dawson replied, looking miserable.

"Then why? Is it something I did? Something I said? Daw, whatever it is, we could have worked it out." Grady hated himself for almost begging, especially since the die was cast. Dawson couldn't change his mind. He was going to leave for four years, and it would never be the same again.

"You need to learn to fly on your own," Dawson replied, his voice strangely thick. "And if I'm here, that won't happen."

"What the fuck does that even mean?"

As angry as Grady was that night, he still saw the raw pain in Dawson's eyes. "I think you know. If I stay, I'll give in. I know I will. And then what happens when you realize down the line that you need to 'find yourself'?"

Oh, Christ. Did Dawson just say what Grady thought he heard? But that would mean... "I won't," Grady replied, in a strangled tone, unable to keep the tears at bay.

Dawson looked so sad. "The only way it works is if you find yourself first."

"And you made this decision about my life for me? Because I'm too young to know my own mind? You think I don't know how I feel?" Heartbreak boomeranged into anger.

"I made this decision about *my* life. We'll both have time to figure out who we really are, what we really want. We can still stay in touch. God, I want to stay in touch. And then, when I get back, if we still want the same things, we'll know." Dawson looked miserable, not trying to hide his tears. "I did it because I don't want to fuck this up, Gray. I couldn't live with that."

"Yeah?" Grady shot back. "Too late. Consider it fucked."

———

"Do you *want* to eat cold barbecue?" Denny called from outside, jarring Grady out of his memories. Grady put the platter on the counter, grabbed the second plate, and hurried out.

"Sorry, sorry," he muttered.

Denny gave him a look but didn't say anything. When the second plate was full, Grady headed back inside while Denny saw to shutting off the smoker. He tried to be useful, bustling around the kitchen to lay out the sandwich buns, sauce, potato salad, chips, and banana pudding as well as plates and silverware.

"Oh man, that smells amazing."

Grady hadn't heard Dawson come down the stairs. He glanced up with an uncertain smile and realized he was blushing. "You know how Uncle Denny likes to cook," Grady replied. "And people have been dropping food off all week—"

He cut off the rest of that sentence, not wanting to spoil Dawson's homecoming with a reminder of Aaron's death. "Anyhow," Grady hurried on before Dawson had a chance to say anything, "I don't imagine they fed you Carolina barbecue in the Army."

"You've got that right." Dawson closed his eyes and breathed deeply, then gave an orgasmic groan that made Grady uncomfortably stiff. Grady turned, hoping to keep his problem from being too obvious.

"There are a ton of cookies. All kinds," Grady rambled on, afraid of silence. "Once everyone heard you were coming home, they started bringing them by. So we're fixed for dessert."

Grady finally ran out of things to say. He looked at Dawson, feeling oddly shy. *This is Daw, the guy you've known all your life. The guy you've been in love with for half your life. Snap out of it!*

"It looks great—but the best thing is just being here," Dawson told him, with an uncertain smile that suggested that he felt the same awkwardness.

"I'm glad you're back," Grady replied, looking away as he felt a little too exposed. "Anyhow, there's cold soda in the fridge and beer. I think Denny figured we'd eat at the picnic table since it's nice out. He just wanted to keep the food in here so Angel didn't get into it." On cue, the dorky Rottweiler scratched at the back door and smashed his nose into the glass.

Dawson laughed. "Yeah, Angel would make quick work of all that meat. Do you remember that time he got the Easter ham—"

"Oh my God, he had that ham down to the bone in seconds," Grady joined in. "I didn't think Denny was going to let him back in the house, ever."

"Well, at least not until Angel stopped puking it all back up because he bolted it too fast," Dawson recalled.

And just like that, it almost felt like old times.

Almost, except that Grady's dad had still been alive that Easter. Dawson's folks too. That was the last holiday they were all together. Before everything changed.

Grady's thoughts must have shown on his face. "Gray—" Dawson started.

"Don't," Grady said, closing his eyes. "Not now. Please. Later. Just not now." Grady had managed to work himself into a decent mood for the first time...*since*. Whatever happened between them now that Dawson was back, Grady just wanted to enjoy tonight, pretend everything was okay, that he wasn't broken inside, that maybe Dawson still wanted him.

"Okay," Dawson replied, his voice low and quiet. "Whatever you need—I'm here."

Tight-lipped, Grady gave a curt nod, then forced a smile. "You'd better fix a plate before Denny comes in after us."

He and Dawson didn't touch, but Grady felt hyper-aware of the other man's presence. They slipped around each other in the familiar kitchen, knowing exactly where to go, when to dodge. They'd always had an uncanny sense of each other, something that came in handy on hunts.

What would it be like, in bed? Grady wondered, not for the first

46

time. He shut down that thought before it could show up on his face. *Not now.*

Thankfully, Dawson didn't push him to talk. They carried their plates and beers out to the table, and Denny passed them on the way in.

"Took you long enough," Denny muttered, shaking his head. "What's the matter—couldn't find the food?" He headed inside, leaving Angel on the porch to finish the kibble in his dish.

Grady and Dawson sat across from each other at the old picnic table. Silence stretched between them, something that used to be natural and comfortable. Now, Grady squirmed, unsure what to say.

"You never did tell me much about college," Dawson broke the impasse.

Grady appreciated the neutral topic. "Yeah. Automotive Technology. Figured it fit in with the business."

The other King legacy was a chain of auto body shops across Transylvania County, started by their great-grandfather. The shops provided a source of income that supported their monster hunting activities, and nearly everyone had a role to play. Grady never had the mechanical aptitude that seemed to come so easily to Dawson. But while Dawson was great with the nuts and bolts side of cars, Grady was good with computers. That made learning the high-tech side of diagnostics and onboard systems easy.

"Computer stuff?"

"Yeah. Not as hands-on as the stuff you like."

Dawson shrugged and took a bite of his sandwich. "Tell me about it."

Grady started talking, nervously babbling at first. Dawson encouraged him with smiles and nods, tossing in questions now and again that showed he was listening. Denny joined them but didn't interrupt. Grady didn't even realize how long he'd been talking until he saw that the other men had cleaned their plates.

"That was probably more than you ever wanted to know," Grady said, self-conscious.

Dawson chuckled. "I'm pretty impressed. Wrenches and grease pits make me feel right at home. Keyboards? Not so much."

"Graduated top of his class, too," Denny added. "He probably didn't mention that."

"Sweet. I'm very proud of you," Dawson said.

Grady searched his gaze and found only sincerity and genuine pride. "Thanks." He felt a blush rise to his cheeks. "You got some promotions that you didn't say much about."

Their opportunities to video call while Dawson was overseas were never predictable and always too short. Neither of them had wanted to talk about work or school.

Dawson shrugged. "What's to say? I was Infantry. Meaning, I shot things. Same thing I did here, different kind of monsters."

His expression told Grady that Dawson had seen things he didn't want to talk about. Considering how much monster hunting experience Dawson had before he went into the Army, it would have taken pretty bad stuff to put that look in his eyes. Grady wasn't sure he wanted to know, but if Dawson ever needed to unburden himself, Grady would find the courage to be his rock.

"Do you think you'll miss it?" Grady had worried that Dawson would find himself at home in the Army, and re-enlist when his tour was over. Part of him feared Dawson would change his mind right up until Dawson received his papers and the flight arrangements were confirmed.

Dawson raised his eyebrows. "The Army? Hell, no. I learned a lot. Met some good people. But if you recall, Kings don't take direction well."

"You don't say," Denny responded drily.

Grady found himself letting go of a fear he didn't even realize he still held. Part of him had feared that Dawson would come home and miss the other life he'd had in the Army—away from the mountain, from monsters, and from Grady.

"I went away for a reason, and I came back for a reason," Dawson said quietly. "I never intended to stay gone." He met Grady's gaze and held it, with a look that made Grady's stomach quiver.

"Why don't I get the banana pudding?" Grady jumped up and bolted into the house before either Dawson or Denny could reply.

He got to the kitchen and leaned back against the refrigerator, careful to stay away from the window, where the others might see. Grady felt everything closing in on him. Sitting and talking to Dawson like nothing had ever changed suddenly seemed wrong when Grady's father was dead because of Grady's failure.

His breath came shallow and fast, and Grady thought he might throw up. The images that haunted his dreams flashed through his mind. The werewolf's fangs sinking deep into his father's shoulder. Deafeningly loud gunshots echoing in the still forest. His father's voice, pleading with Grady to shoot him or leave the gun so he could do it himself. And then, another shot fired, and blood. So much blood.

Grady's vision started to gray out, and black spots danced in front of his eyes. Everything he had eaten threatened to come back up as his stomach twisted into knots. His dry mouth made it hard to swallow as bile began to rise. Grady struggled to breathe, as his heartbeat thundered in his ears. He slid down and sat on the floor.

"It's okay." Dawson's voice broke into the din of Grady's thoughts. "I've got you."

Grady shook his head. "It's not okay. Never be okay. All my fault."

"Shh," Dawson coaxed, lowering himself to the floor to sit next to Grady. "Breathe."

"I let him down. Should have seen it coming. Wasn't fast enough."

Dawson moved in front of Grady and gently took him by the shoulders, staring into his eyes with determined focus. "Stay with me, Gray. We can talk about the details later. Right now, I just need you to breathe. Can you do that? Breathe with me. In-two-three-four. Hold. Out-two-three-four. Again."

Dawson breathed with him, over and over, until Grady's panic lessened. Once his heart stopped pounding, and he could draw a full breath, embarrassment took over.

"I'm sorry," Grady murmured, self-conscious. He wanted to crawl into a hole and never come out. *I should have stayed in my room. I'm fucking up Dawson's first day home.*

"You've got nothing to be sorry about." Dawson still held Grady by the shoulders.

Grady slumped. "I just get...overwhelmed sometimes."

"Gray, it's only been a week." Dawson stayed close as if he realized how much Grady needed the anchoring touch. "Losing someone under normal circumstances takes time to deal with. No one gets over it that fast. And you didn't have *normal* circumstances."

"I'm screwing this all up," Grady said, unable to meet Dawson's gaze.

"I won't let you," Dawson assured him. "We're going to take things slow. There's no rush, no pressure. We've got all the time in the world."

Grady wanted to believe Dawson with all his heart. At the same time, a malicious whisper in the back of his brain warned that Dawson wouldn't be patient forever. Once he found out how badly broken Grady really was, why would he stay?

"Do you want some water?" Dawson asked. "Is there anything I can get for you to help take the edge off?"

Grady shook his head. Since his father had died on the hunt for a monster, going to a doctor for help to get through the aftermath hadn't been an option. Hunt-related injuries got treated by a couple of crusty old retired doctors who knew about what lurked in the shadows. They were competent to handle pretty much everything short of major surgery, but they weren't big on the touchy-feely side of medicine.

Asking for more than a handful of sleeping pills—let alone something for anxiety or depression—would have gotten Grady a lecture about "manning up." He couldn't bear that scorn, not when Grady felt certain those who knew what really happened would never look at him the same way again.

"Just water," he managed. Dawson let go of him to fill a glass, and Grady missed the contact immediately.

"Here," Dawson said gently as he hunkered down next to Grady and held the drink out.

Grady drank it all, trying to collect himself, and handed the glass back. He tried to stand, and Dawson steadied him when he almost fell.

"Need to take the pudding outside."

"The pudding will be fine."

Grady shook his head stubbornly. "Can't have a 'welcome home' party without it," he said, trying to divert attention from his panic attack.

"Oh yeah? Says who?" Dawson joked, clearly understanding without needing to be told that Grady wanted to talk about anything except what just occurred.

"Everyone," Grady replied, as banter came naturally once more.

"Well, 'everyone' is going to have to get their own banana pudding because this one is for you, me, and Denny," Dawson said, grabbing the chilled serving dish out of the refrigerator. Grady took the bowls and spoons from the table, needing to do something useful.

Denny didn't say anything when they came back to the table, but he gave Grady a concerned once-over and shared a look with Dawson that Grady couldn't interpret. Unwilling to think about anything except the pudding, Grady accepted a generous helping as Denny served the dessert. He focused on the homemade comfort food. Banana pudding had a place on the table for so many special occasions and holidays that just smelling and tasting it sent a warm feeling through Grady.

Until he realized his dad would never be part of one of those celebrations again.

Grady pushed the bowl away. "It was a big serving," he murmured. "Really good, but I can't eat anymore."

Denny nodded without saying anything.

Dawson smiled. "I'll put a piece of plastic wrap over it and stick it in the fridge in case you get hungry later."

"Sounds good," Grady replied, although it took all his willpower not to throw up. He stood. "I'm going to go put everything away, and then lie down if that's okay. My head is killing me."

"Don't worry about the kitchen," Dawson assured him. "Denny and I can handle it. Kinda like KP duty," he added with a wink.

Grady murmured his thanks and took off, worried about the expressions he might see if he looked back. When he reached his room, he dropped onto his bed and only barely managed to stifle a sob.

God, I'm useless. I've been waiting for so long for this day, and look at the mess I've made. He turned his back to the door, buried his head in his pillow, and let the tears flow silently until he fell asleep.

———

WHEN HE WOKE, IT WAS LIGHT OUTSIDE, MEANING GRADY HAD SLEPT the whole night in his clothes. He groaned as he sat up, feeling like shit. He hadn't brushed his teeth, and his breath probably smelled like summer roadkill. A glance at the clock told him it was already ten. *Time to face the music.*

Grady figured Dawson and Denny had already gotten their showers, and he slipped into the bathroom without running into anyone. The shower loosened sore muscles gone stiff from sleeping in an awkward position. Brushing his teeth restored a little more of his humanity. He made an effort to style his hair and shaved, figuring he could at least fake looking like a normal human being. Then he plastered on his best smile and headed for the kitchen.

Dawson sat at the table, nursing a cup of coffee and absently petting Angel as he stared out the window. An empty bowl of cereal was pushed out of the way to one side. He looked up and smiled when Grady entered. Angel wagged and ran over to greet him, and Grady leaned down to scratch the dog's ears.

"Glad you're up," Dawson said. "There's fresh coffee. Denny and I drank the first pot so that one is barely an hour old. Fresh bacon is in the pan on the stove. Other than that, you probably know more about the breakfast options than I do."

Grady knew Denny had planned to do waffles for Dawson's first morning home and guessed his breakdown postponed the celebration breakfast. He knew neither of the other men would care, but Grady couldn't help feeling it added another failure to his tally.

He poured a cup of coffee, fixed it the way he liked, and decided toast was probably the safest bet. While he waited for the slices to pop up, Grady munched a couple of strips of bacon. Then he buttered the toast, slathered on some of the neighbor's homemade blackberry jam, and sat across from Dawson.

"Still drink it with cream and sugar, like always," Dawson noted. "I learned to drink it plain black because that's what was available, but I won't turn down sugar, now that I'm back in civilization."

"You're on Cunanoon Mountain," Grady replied with a faint smile. "If you were looking for civilization, you got off at the wrong stop."

"Nope. I'm right where I belong."

Grady braced himself for questions about yesterday's disaster. Instead, Dawson turned his focus back to the window, sparing Grady the feeling of being watched.

"I thought it could be fun to take the Mustang out for a spin since it's a nice day. Drive around, see what's changed since I've been gone," he said, making the suggestion sound off-handed.

"There's not much new, but I'm sure you've been looking forward to getting behind the wheel again." As much as Grady hated the thought of Dawson leaving again after just getting home, he knew that some fresh air would do him good.

"Want to come along?" Dawson asked, turning to look at Grady and giving him the smile that always made Grady's heart stutter. The smile reached his eyes, letting Grady know that Dawson really did want company.

"Sure. I'm out of practice at conversation though," Grady warned.

"I haven't exactly been hanging out with the philosophy club," Dawson replied, chuckling. "I guarantee you'll be an upgrade."

They cleaned up their dishes, left a note for Denny, and went out to the barn. Dawson grinned ear-to-ear when he saw the cloth-draped sports car parked in the corner.

"Oh, Sally-girl, did you miss me?" Dawson made a bee-line to the car, and Grady helped him remove the protective cover. The vintage Mustang looked showroom-new, gleaming from the recent wax job Grady had given it two weeks ago as a welcome-home present.

Dawson picked up on that right away. "You waxed her?"

Grady nodded. "Denny and I made sure she got driven—carefully —and kept up on the battery and the tires. Denny also added new weapons, protective charms, and other stuff to the lockbox under the back seat whenever he got a new stash. I waxed her every few months." He shrugged. "Wanted to make sure she was ready when you got back."

Grady didn't mention that caring for the car had made him feel closer to Dawson. Sometimes he just snuck out and sat in the car, thinking about his favorite memories of their time together. There was no way he intended to admit that.

"Thank you." Dawson's voice sounded a little awestruck. "That means a lot."

Grady smiled. "Well, Sally's not just any car. She deserves to be treated like a queen."

The bright red Mustang Boss 429 had a wide black stripe over the hood. The powerful engine was designed for stock car racing, and installed in a limited number of street-legal cars to satisfy NASCAR rules. Dawson had rebuilt Sally from a junked hulk he had found in a salvage yard. Grady remembered keeping Dawson company during those evenings and weekends that it took to bring the old car back to life.

Dawson settled in behind the wheel and let out a satisfied sigh. "Christ, I've missed this," he said, with a glance toward Grady that included him in that statement and sent a warm thrill to Grady's belly.

"Then let's get the hell out of the barn," Grady replied. "And you can see all the things that didn't change while you've been gone."

Dawson took the curves down the mountain a little too fast, as always, and Grady could see the enjoyment on his face as the Mustang hugged the road, handling like the race car she was. The bass rumble of the engine thrummed, almost drowning out the classic rock songs blasting from the radio.

Grady sang along at the top of his voice, off-key and faking the words. He could pretend they were back in high school, that nothing had changed, and everyone would still be waiting when they got home. Change came slowly on Cunanoon Mountain, so he'd been telling the truth when he said there wasn't much new worth commenting on. A few old buildings burned or got torn down, and here and there a shop, gas station, or restaurant sprang up in their wake. Nothing newsworthy.

They pulled into Connor's Corner, a 1950s-era drive-up restaurant that had been the after-school hang out for several generations. Big national chains had fast food restaurants near the Interstate, but in the valley, almost everything remained local. Grady liked the chocolate milkshakes and corn dogs, while Dawson always craved their pizza burgers, and swore the hand-cut French fries were the best, anywhere. Except for a fresh coat of paint every so often, the place looked the same as always.

"Gotta hit all the stops on my come-back tour," Dawson told him with a grin as they lounged at a cement picnic table at the edge of the parking lot. A few people waved when they saw Dawson, and two or three wandered up to say hello and welcome him back. Grady savored his milkshake and tried to stay in the here-and-now, shutting out the nightmares and not worrying about the future.

The bright sunny day, mild temperatures, and loud music made it easy to be in a good mood. When they left Connor's Corner, Dawson took a few turns, and Grady knew right away where they were headed, although he hadn't been there since Dawson left for the Army.

"Bootlegger's Run" was what all the locals called a deserted stretch of State Route 215 that hugged the mountains, then opened into a flat, two-mile strip of road perfect for racing. Back during Prohibition, young men raced their souped-up cars here when they weren't hauling moonshine and outrunning the authorities. There was no place better to open up the Mustang and let her fly.

"Whoo-hoo!" Dawson let out a yell of jubilation as he floored the pedal and watched the needle climb. Grady loved the thrilled terror that roiled his stomach and stirred his cock. If they hit anything, they'd be dead before the pieces of the car stopped rolling. But cheating death and living to tell about it gave a buzz moonshine couldn't match.

Lights strobed a good distance behind, and a police siren wailed. Dawson cursed under his breath, and Grady tried to ease his white-knuckled grip on the armrest. Grady recognized that momentary flash of an expression that crossed Dawson's face as he debated running for it. The Sheriff's car would not be able to catch them. But there wasn't another car like Sally anywhere near here, and everyone knew who owned her.

"Fuck," Dawson muttered, slowing the Mustang and pulling over to the side of the road. They sat with their hands visible as Sheriff Beau Rollins sauntered up, sunlight glinting from the aviator sunglasses that hid his eyes beneath the broad brim of his hat.

Rollins was a wolf shifter, and so were most of his deputies. Not a werewolf—his ability to change form had nothing to do with the phase of the moon. Like his wolf, Rollins had thick russet hair, a powerful build, and brown eyes that flashed yellow in the right light.

"Guess this means you're my problem again, Dawson King." He glanced at Grady. "Well, shit. Butch and Sundance ride again."

Grady kept his face neutral. Dawson greeted the lawman with a grin.

"It's good to be home, Sheriff," he said. "Can I help you with something?"

Rollins's sour expression suggested a bad bout of indigestion. "Do you have any idea how fast you were going?"

Grady knew they were well over ninety, not that he was going to volunteer that information.

"I was watching the road, sir. Didn't take my eyes off it to look at the instrument panel."

"One-oh-three, that's how fast. I could take your license, impound your car, and throw you both in jail—plus a hefty fine, and I've got a mind to do just that."

Grady leaned forward with a smile. "Isn't that going to make it hard to hold the parade?"

Rollins glared at him. "What parade?"

Grady hoped he could still pull off wide-eyed and innocent. He was out of practice since he hadn't almost been arrested since Dawson went into the Army.

"The Welcome Home, Hero" parade," Grady went on. "For Dawson. I mean, local boy earns a Purple Heart saving a squadron after he'd been badly wounded…it was on the news. You know how much North Carolina loves its folks in uniform. I assumed the mayor had already talked to you about providing escort." He widened his eyes as if he'd just told a secret. "Unless he meant to have the State Police do the honors."

Rollins looked ready to chew nails. "If anyone is going to escort a parade in my jurisdiction, it's gonna be me and my deputies. Not a bunch of Staties from out of town."

"I imagine the TV news will be there," Grady continued. "The mayor's already sent out the press release. It'll be a nice photo op for the department—unless the man of the hour is in jail."

Dawson wisely kept his mouth shut. Grady tried for his most angelic expression. Finally, Rollins caved.

"Fuck my life," he muttered. "I will let you off with a warning—just this once, you hear me? Since the road had no traffic on it, and you just got back from the service. But that's it. Do not try my patience."

"Thank you," Grady replied. "Thank you so much."

"Get out of here," Rollins snapped. "At a legal speed. Understand?"

Both Dawson and Grady nodded solemnly. Rollins stared them down for another minute, then stalked off to his cruiser.

Dawson put the Mustang into gear and pulled out slowly, staying just under the speed limit for several miles as Rollins followed them in his patrol car. Dawson let his speed slip lower and lower, still careful to stay above the forty-five mile-an-hour minimum, but far slower than the stated limit of seventy—or the average of at least eighty most locals generally drove it at.

"Please tell me you made up the whole parade thing."

"I might have embellished it," Grady admitted. "There's a reception this weekend with cake down at the community center. But I imagine there'll be a photographer from the paper, and if you drive Sally real slow on the way, it's sorta like a parade when traffic backs up behind you."

After several miles, Rollins pulled out around them, passing with a roar of his engine and vanishing over the horizon.

"If he has a stroke, it's going to be your fault," Grady chided with mischief in his eyes.

"He's wound a bit tight, even for a wolf."

"Actually, most people in town rather like him."

"He's got it in for our family." Not taking any chances that Rollins was setting a trap for them ahead, Dawson did a U-turn and headed back the way they came, above the speed limit but not flat out like before.

"After what our dads did to him back in high school, do you blame him?"

"That was a long time ago."

Grady just gave Dawson a look. "It's not the kind of thing you forget."

The story was a bona fide King family legend. Back in high school, Ethan and Aaron King had decided to teach Rollins and his shifter-jock friends a lesson for being assholes. The two King brothers had taken Rollins out drinking and gotten him black-out drunk without losing their own faculties.

When Rollins woke up, he was naked as a jaybird, lying on the cold steel of the veterinarian's operating room, with his balls wrapped in gauze and a brochure on *Care for your Neutered Pet* lying on his chest.

While that was long before the internet, Polaroid photos were rumored to exist. Even though no surgery had been done, Rollins hadn't discovered that without a panicked call to the vet—and a lot of ribbing afterward. Needless to say, relations between the sheriff and the county's most prominent monster-hunting family had been frosty since that point.

"Rollins isn't a complete dick," Dawson admitted. He shifted without hesitation, pure muscle memory, and the Mustang's engine changed tone with each gear in a song that had often lulled Grady to sleep on long drives. "He's been good back-up when we've needed him on a hunt."

"Probably because he knows everyone would suspect him if one of the Kings got shot in the back," Grady replied, but he couldn't keep the smile out of his voice.

This right here was part of what he loved about Dawson, and what he had missed like a phantom limb these past four years. The Mustang roaring along back roads, breaking a few rules for a good cause, the adrenaline of the hunt, and then the sweet relief of living to hunt another day, topped off by a couple of cold beers.

The only way it could be any better was if Dawson gave him a sign —any sign—that he intended for them to be more than what they were.

In his heart, Grady knew that what had begun as hero worship had tempered and matured, built on long experience, into something deep and real. He owned the fact that he'd been in love with Dawson for a very long time. In their last few video calls before Dawson left for home, although they had to talk around the point because of military eavesdroppers, Grady had clearly heard a promise for them to take this thing between them to the next level.

So why hadn't Dawson made a move on him, when they'd been alone all afternoon?

He's said all the right things, Grady thought. *He's probably still jet-lagged and getting his wits together being back in the States. And my little freak-out last night certainly didn't help.*

I just need to be patient. I've waited this long. I can wait a while longer until we've both got our feet under us. Until I'm not such a hot mess.

But please...not too long.

5

DAWSON

"Colt told me about a haunted house that's giving its owners a fit. A nuisance, really. I thought I'd go over and take a look after lunch. Want to come with me?"

He made the offer like it was no big deal, but found himself holding his breath. Two days had passed since Grady's panic attack, and to Dawson's relief, there hadn't been a repeat.

Dawson also felt relieved that he hadn't had one of his nightmares since he'd been home. It was only a matter of time, and he'd have the whole house awake with his shouts. Even more importantly, he hadn't had another dream of a Black Shuck. Dawson knew the scars of what he had survived ran deep and didn't ever completely fade, just like with Grady's trauma.

Still, he had to believe they could get past this and move on. They were both broken right now, but they would heal. And maybe, by healing together, be even stronger than before. Dawson hung onto that hope.

"A hunt?" Grady sounded skeptical. "You want me to hunt with you?"

Dawson's heart ached at the mix of eagerness and doubt in

Grady's eyes. He knew the other man wanted to go, and also feared that he might not be up to the challenge. Or worse, feared that he might get Dawson hurt or killed.

"I wouldn't really call it a 'hunt' exactly," Dawson replied, trying to sound off-handed. "More of a banishment. Think of it as a public service."

"Did they try a priest?" Grady remained skeptical.

"They brought in Father Keene from the Catholic Church down in the valley. Probably had him say a couple of prayers and splash some holy water around," Dawson said. "Keene doesn't believe in any of the paranormal stuff, not like old Father Kinsella."

"I'm not saying that Father Kinsella was old," Grady deadpanned, "but I think he attended Jesus's bar mitzvah."

Dawson chuckled, pleased to see a glimpse of Grady's sense of humor. "Could be. Anyhow, Keene probably did some New Age-y blessings and called it a day. This might just take a little old-school banishing, and we gain ourselves another satisfied customer."

"I'm not sure Catholic priests do New Age."

"You know what I mean."

Grady hesitated, and Dawson imagined that he could see all of the other man's internal arguments pro and con flash across his face.

"Sure," Grady said at last. "Sounds like fun."

Uncle Denny had gone into town on an errand, so Dawson made sure Angel had kibble and water, then headed for the Mustang, where Grady waited in the front seat. Dawson had already packed a bag with everything they might need for a banishment—or a straight-up exorcism—although he hoped it didn't come to that.

It was on the tip of Dawson's tongue to ask about the hunts Grady had gone on while he'd been gone. Then he remembered, just in time, that Grady had hunted with his dad and Denny. He didn't want to tank Grady's mood by mentioning his father.

"How many of the cars you get out here need all the computerized stuff you learned about?" Dawson steered the conversation toward safe territory. Grady hadn't gone into work since Dawson had been home, which meant he was probably on leave.

"More than you'd think." Grady looked relieved to have a neutral topic to fill the silence. "Pretty much everything from 1980 on has some computerized components. Anything after 1990 has a lot. There are plenty of old cars still running out here, but lots of newer ones, too."

"And you can do all that, with the tech at the shop?" Dawson didn't pay too much attention to anything that didn't require a lift or a creeper.

Grady smiled, and the hint of pride in his expression made Dawson happy. "They bought a new diagnostic unit since I knew how to run it. Now we can do almost everything, so people don't have to run back to the dealers in Asheville."

"Nice. I bet that paid for itself pretty quick. It'll be fun working together again."

Grady brightened as if he hadn't thought about that. "Maybe we can get them to work out our schedules so we can ride together."

"Pretty sure since our last name is over the door, we can figure something out," Dawson assured him.

Everything in Dawson wanted to reach out and take Grady's hand, twine their fingers together, pull him close. When Dawson had imagined their reunion, before he shipped out, he'd thought about sweeping Grady off his feet with a passionate kiss. Then Aaron died, and Dawson knew it wasn't the right time for a dramatic entrance.

Still, knowing that going slow was the right thing to do didn't soothe the need Dawson felt to hold Grady close. And his dick didn't understand in the least. At times, Dawson felt just as hopelessly frustrated as he had before he went away, tormented by an over-developed sense of honor that was the ultimate cock-blocker.

Doing the right thing takes longer, pays off in the end, he told himself. The fact that Grady hadn't been flirting with him beyond a few longing glances told Dawson that the other man wasn't ready for more, not just yet.

Coming straight out and saying that he was holding off because he didn't think Grady was in the right headspace wasn't likely to work. Grady would be hurt and angry. Dawson hadn't forgotten

Grady's rage over his decision to join the Army, and his well-aimed barbs that Dawson had no right to make decisions for him, or on his behalf, without consulting him.

This isn't the same. I'm not making an unbreakable four-year commit-ment that sends me overseas. Maybe in a few weeks, a month or two, we can start "dating." That can't happen soon enough for me.

"Jamison's B&B?" Grady looked confused when Dawson parked the Mustang near a colorful old Victorian home, a favorite with the tourists who enjoyed hiking the area's nature trails. "Since when is it haunted?"

"Colt told me Sarah Jamison died a few months ago and left the place to her son," Dawson said.

"Yeah, I think I heard something about that. But who's haunting it? No one ever said it had a ghost problem before."

"Apparently, the original owner. Or at least, that's what Sarah's son thinks. He tracked down Colt yesterday and asked if someone could come by." Dawson grabbed his gear bag from the backseat and joined Grady at the bottom of the steps to the front porch.

A *"Vacancies"* sign in the window suggested that the ghost hadn't been good for business.

A red-headed man in his late thirties answered the door, wearing a Captain America T-shirt over jeans. "Are you looking for a room?" He sounded friendly and a little desperate.

Dawson flashed a smile. "I'm Dawson King, and this is Grady King. Colt Summers said you had a haunting problem?"

Most people in these parts had heard of the King family, even if they'd never personally had a run-in with the supernatural. While the family turned down all requests for interviews or contracts for paranormal investigator shows, word got out to everyone who needed to know.

"I'm Patrick Jamison—Pat. Thank you so much for coming. Please, come in." He stepped aside to allow them entrance.

The old home had been beautifully restored. The rich dark wood of the staircase, floor, and chair rails went perfectly with the wine-hued velvet draperies and emerald-colored area rugs. Dawson looked around, impressed. Not that he'd ever need to get a room when he was so close to home, but the B&B lived up to its ads.

"Have a seat. Can I get you some coffee or water?" Pat made a perfect host, even though Dawson picked up an edge of nervousness in his voice and movements.

"We're fine, thank you. Tell us what's going on," Dawson prompted.

He and Grady settled onto a high-backed sofa covered in red velvet. None of the stiff, formal furnishings looked comfortable, although they made a pretty, period-authentic room.

Pat took a seat in an armchair across from them. He clasped his hands in front of him as if he were trying not to fidget. "My parents bought the B&B when I was five. I've spent my whole life in this house, and I watched them build up the business through good times and bad. When my dad had a heart attack ten years ago, I stepped into a bigger role, helping mom keep things going. And when she passed on a few months ago, the inn came to me."

"It's a beautiful place," Grady said with an encouraging smile.

"Thank you. I've poured my soul into this business," Pat confessed. "It's not just my livelihood; it's a little piece of local history that I'm helping to keep alive. The Walker family made a fortune from lumber back at the turn of the last century, and Edwin Walker built the house for his bride, who was coming all the way from Raleigh. He wanted to impress her and make her feel at home in the 'wilderness.'"

Dawson had driven past the elaborately-painted house all his life but had never heard its history. *Obviously, it hasn't had a longstanding ghost problem, or we'd have known.*

"Did she like it?' Grady asked, and Dawson knew his cousin was doing his best to set Pat at ease.

"Oh yes. By all accounts, Edwin and Naomi were very happy here their whole lives," Pat replied. "She came from a wealthy family, and they often visited their friends, the Vanderbilts, up in Asheville."

"I'm guessing the hauntings are new?" Dawson asked.

Pat nodded. "At least since my family owned the place. I never saw anything, and Mom never mentioned any problems. I think I know why the problems started—but I don't know how to make it stop."

Dawson found himself liking the man, who appeared to be genuinely distraught. Pat was about Grady's height, but with a softer body, as if he spent a bit too much time in the kitchen. Dawson noticed a wedding ring and wondered whether both partners were involved with the B&B.

"Edwin Walker was a strict Presbyterian," Pat continued. "He wasn't much of a drinker, didn't smoke, and would only play cards if no gambling was involved. But he drew a strict line on what he considered to be morality. To make a long story short, the hauntings didn't begin until my husband moved in after our wedding."

A dark-haired man came in from the kitchen and stood behind Pat's chair, placing a hand on his shoulder. Pat reached up and tangled their fingers together. Dawson felt his heart squeeze.

That's what I want someday. He didn't dare look at Grady, but he felt very aware of his presence a few inches away on the couch.

"Hi, I'm Jason," the newcomer said. He looked a few years younger than Pat and wore a T-shirt from a local wilderness outfitter and jeans that looked like they had seen a few hikes. "And I guess, technically, this is all my fault."

Pat gave him a gently reproving look. "No, it's not. Edwin is dead and gone. He had a right to live his life, but he doesn't have a right to dictate ours."

Pat turned his attention back to Dawson and Grady. "Mom completely approved, in case you're wondering. All the time we dated, I went up to Brevard, where Jason lived, because there was more to do there, and we had more privacy. Our wedding was planned before Mom got sick. She went quickly, a total surprise. But she gave us her blessing, and told me not to put off my happiness mourning her."

He raised the back of his free hand to wipe a tear from his eye, and Jason squeezed his fingers. "So we got married on schedule, and

Jason moved in. That was a month ago. After that, the hauntings started."

"What kind of things are happening?" Dawson leaned forward, intrigued. He'd run into ghosts who stuck around for a lot of reasons and plenty of kinds of unfinished business, but never one who took it upon himself to be the chastity police.

"Edwin didn't act up while we were moving Jason's things into the house," Pat said. "Maybe he thought Jason was a friend or a brother. He didn't even seem to notice that we moved his personal things into my room. But that first night that we slept in the bed together—and we were so tired, all we did was sleep—the problems started.

"The clock on the mantle in our room wouldn't stop chiming for a solid hour." Jason took up the story.

"We couldn't figure out why, since it never did that before. Then in the morning the covers were completely off the bed—not like they were kicked off, but like someone pulled them off in the opposite direction."

"Shit," Grady muttered.

"We didn't know what was really going on that first night, but we thought it might have somehow been a fluke," Pat said. "The next night, the temperature dropped low enough that we got frost on the inside of the bedroom windows—just the bedroom we share. And the covers got pulled off again."

"It's gotten worse each night," Jason said quietly. "Books pulled off shelves. Knickknacks knocked to the ground and broken. Things go missing—car keys, jewelry, my e-reader—and then show up some-place we'd never have put them."

"We thought we had a prankster spirit at first," Pat said. "A mischievous energy that attached itself to one of our guests or some-thing." At their surprised looks, Pat managed a smile. "Hey, I can Google as well as anyone. And I've watched that one TV show enough to know about salt and ghosts."

"So we put down salt lines all around the walls of the bedroom," Jason said. And we made sure we wore jewelry that had silver and iron. And for a few days, the problem stopped. Just to be careful, we smudged with sage, said prayers, even had a priest come over to 'bless the house.'"

"And then it started up again," Pat said. "We lit candles. We put crystals in the corners of our room. Hung bundles of protective plants over the windows and door. Played CDs of Gregorian chants in Latin and Tibetan sacred drumming. Neither of us is very religious, but we even found a recording of the whole Latin Mass and played it. Things would get better for a day or so, and then pick back up, worse than before. The problems only ever happened in our room."

"We weren't getting any sleep. And while the guests didn't seem to hear or see anything odd or even notice, Pat and I just weren't coping well," Jason added. "Plus, we'd just gotten married, and we couldn't get any 'downtime.'" He blushed, but Dawson could empathize.

"We had no idea why this was happening or why it was targeting us. We thought about closing down the inn, even though people had reservations. The ghost hadn't bothered the guests, but we were afraid someone would get hurt," Jason went on. "And then I remembered someone I knew in Asheville who said she could talk to ghosts. So I invited her to come visit. She picked up on the ghost's energy right away. That's how we found out who he was and why he was angry."

"Jenny—the medium—told Edwin to go into the light, that he was dead and gone and needed to leave us alone," Pat said, and Dawson could see the anger in the other man's eyes. "And he refused."

"When did that happen?" Grady asked, looking completely caught up in the story.

"Four days ago. Edwin went away for forty-eight hours. Then he came back—and he was pissed," Pat replied. "Something snatched the blankets off the bed while we were sleeping. I don't mean pulled on them. I mean ripped the blankets and sheets off even though they were tucked in at the bottom—all in one movement—and then threw them across the room."

"And then something did this." Jason pulled at the collar of his T-shirt to reveal livid bruises in the shape of fingerprints around his neck. They had started to fade but still looked painful.

"Holy fuck," Dawson muttered.

"We can't just leave," Pat said, and now that Dawson understood what was going on, he could see the stress and exhaustion in the man's face. "We have guests. Thankfully, no one else has been bothered. But what happens when we get a gay couple staying with us? And how long until Jason or I get seriously injured?"

"Since we can't both leave, we did the closest thing. I got us a room at the chain hotel out by the highway. We take turns having one of us sleep there, and the other comes into the B&B to run things. I can't tell you how increasingly angry I am that I can't sleep with my own husband because of a prudish prick of a dead guy." Anger colored Jason's features.

"That was when I ran into Colt and told him what was going on," Pat said, smoothing a hand back through his hair in a nervous gesture. "We'd run out of ideas. I'd heard of your family, sure, but I thought you just went after monsters. Not ghosts."

"We're sort of a one-size-fits-all spook exterminator," Dawson joked.

"Can you help?" Pat asked, and this time, Dawson knew he didn't imagine the desperation in the man's voice. "If I have to choose between my livelihood and my husband, Jason wins, hands down. But I love this place, even if it was built by a homophobic old coot. I'd like to keep it if we can. It's my family's legacy."

Grady and Dawson traded glances. Dawson could see how much Grady wanted to help, and he felt the same tug. Pat and Jason deserved better, and Edwin needed to suck it up and cross over.

"We'll give it our best shot," Dawson promised. "From what you've said, you did a lot of the right things—sage, salt, crystals. There are ways to power up those protections and make it uncomfortable for Edwin."

"Are your guests here now?" Grady asked.

Pat shook his head. "Since you were coming, we arranged for them to all have free tickets for the arts and crafts show. It's a pretty big deal, and there's live music and food trucks there tonight, so it should keep them out for several more hours."

"If you can direct us to the room where the problem is, we'll deal with it," Dawson said. "And we need you and Jason to stay down here —or even out on the porch. It sounds like Edwin's a sore loser, and if he thinks he's really going to get banished, he might strike out at you if you're close."

"Do you know which room Edwin and Naomi used when they lived here?" Grady asked.

"From what we've found in old pictures, the front right bedroom," Pat replied. "It's a guest room now. I always liked the rear left room because of the view of the backyard, so that was mine growing up and now it's ours."

"Are there any objects in your bedroom that might have either belonged to Edwin or been in the house when Edwin owned it?" Grady asked.

"I know B&Bs are supposed to be full of antiques—and we've got them in the guest rooms and the public areas," Pat replied. "But after growing up with old stuff, I promised myself that my room would be all new furniture. So all of the pieces in our room are new."

"Except for the clock," Jason said. "You liked the way it looked on the mantle."

Pat nodded. "I should have thought of that. It's old. I don't know if it belonged to Edwin, but it's been around for as long as I can remember. I thought my parents bought it." He looked from Dawson to Grady. "Do you think that's it?"

"It's a place to start," Dawson said. "Any other knickknacks, artwork, rugs, lamps he might have owned?"

Both men shook their heads. "Everything else we either bought ourselves or together. Except for the clock."

Pat and Jason went out to sit on the porch. Dawson and Grady took their gear upstairs, already expecting trouble. Dawson had pulled out a canister of salt mixed with iron filings and other protective plant powders. Both of them had iron knives to disrupt ghostly energy. Dawson also had a shotgun with shells filled with rock salt and iron pellets, which he hoped was a last resort. He had the iron knife in his hand, the salt in his jacket pocket, and the shotgun on a strap slung over his shoulder.

Even though they hadn't done a hunt together in four years, old habits fell into place easily. Dawson took point, with Grady moving backward behind him, covering their rear.

Dawson and Grady exchanged an unspoken acknowledgment, and Dawson turned the knob, opening the bedroom door.

The room was tidy, with comfortable furnishings and decorations that reflected the personalities of the owners. Superhero figures decorated the shelves, while framed photographs of local scenery hung on the wall. A mahogany four-poster king-size bed dominated the room, and the navy blue of the comforter carried over to the curtains, the accent rug, and the upholstery on two armchairs near a fireplace that still looked functional.

On the mantel sat a wooden clock in a curved chestnut case. The beautiful woodwork caught Dawson's eye right away. The clock face had yellowed with age, but its gold numerals were easy to read. Dawson could understand why Pat had wanted the piece, but it had to go.

Grady poured out salt in a circle and stepped inside. Dawson handed him the shotgun.

"Cover me," Dawson said as he moved toward the fireplace and set down a semicircle around the hearth. He took out a small can of lighter fluid and a pack of matches, then took a deep breath to ground himself, and reached for the clock.

The temperature in the room dropped from comfortable to freezing, and Dawson saw his breath send white puffs into the air. A figure took shape, indistinct at first, then coming into focus to reveal an older man dressed in a fine suit from the late 1800s. The ghost of Edwin Walker lunged toward Dawson, only to be forced back by the salt.

"Get out of my house! Take your abominations with you!" Edwin came at Dawson again, hurling himself against the invisible barrier and recoiling with a shriek.

"Hey, asshole!" Grady yelled, trying to draw Edwin off. "Come over here and say that!"

Edwin's image blinked out of sight as Dawson set both hands on the clock, lifting it from its place, and then hurled it into the fireplace. It smashed into pieces, splintering the case, cracking the glass, and leaving the brass gears inside protruding like entrails.

Dawson hunkered down next to the hearth, sloshing the broken clock with accelerant. A frigid wind arose from nowhere, whipping through the room. It blew out his match and threatened to scatter the thick protective salt line.

"You are just like them. I will not tolerate this in my house."

"This isn't your house anymore, asshole." The shotgun boomed, pelting the paneling. "Hurry!" Grady shouted. "I'd rather not shoot the place up."

Dawson folded in on himself, sheltering the new matches as they lit, and then tossing them into the fireplace, where the lighter fluid roared into flame. A new gust of wind tore through the room, eroding the salt line that protected Dawson and the fireplace.

"Put out that fire, or he dies."

Dawson wheeled to see Edwin's ghost, fueled by rage, looking almost solid as he choked Grady, hands locked around his throat just like the bruises on Jason's neck. From the panicked expression on Grady's face, Edwin's ghostly grip was strong enough to do the job. Grady twisted and kicked, but nothing had an effect on the spirit. The shotgun lay on the floor where Grady had dropped it.

"I can't put out the fire without my extinguisher," Dawson said, hands raised in front of him in appeasement. "It's in my bag. Please, don't hurt him." He met Grady's desperate gaze and hoped his partner could read his intent.

Dawson edged closer to the bag, as the flames crackled on old varnish and dry wood. He reached the bag as Grady bucked and fought even harder, drawing Edwin's full, furious attention.

Dawson dove for the gun, rolled and came up firing, sending a blast of salt and iron through the vengeful ghost, who disappeared with a scream of frustration.

Grady collapsed, gasping for air, red-faced and wide-eyed.

Dawson's military training kicked in, and he ignored the instinct to run to Grady and ensure that he was safe. "Hang onto this," he said with a lopsided grin as he tossed the shotgun to Grady, who caught it without missing a beat.

Charred wood, melted glass, and twisted brass remained as the fire burned down. For good measure, Dawson fed the flames another squirt of lighter fluid and watched them leap high toward the flue. He grabbed an iron poker from the stand on the hearth and smashed the pieces into ash and powder.

The room warmed quickly. Dawson remained watching the fire, unwilling to believe it was really over until the last bits of the clock were gone.

He knew, somehow, that Grady and I are gay. He came after us like he went for Pat and Jason. God, what an asshole.

One instant seared into Dawson's mind—seeing Grady choking in Edwin's grip, and fearing he would be too late to save him.

"Hey." Grady had come up behind Dawson. He still held the shotgun, but Dawson doubted Edwin would be back.

"Hey, yourself. Are you okay?" Dawson kept staring into the fire, gathering his control.

"Might have some bruises. For a ghost, that guy had a hella strong grip." Grady's light tone couldn't hide a new rasp to his voice.

"Sorry I wasn't faster."

"My fault for letting him knock the gun out of my hands. I didn't think he'd be that strong."

Dawson shrugged, not willing to share the blame. "You did fine. We're both rusty." He gave a bitter chuckle. "So much for an easy hunt."

Grady nudged him with an elbow. "Come on. We need to tell Pat and Jason it's safe to come in. And explain the buckshot in their paneling."

The two of them headed downstairs and found the inn's owners pacing on the porch.

"We heard gunfire. Are you alright?" Pat asked, worry clear on his face. Jason stopped pacing, and his gaze raked over them, hesitating at Grady's throat where bruises were already forming.

"Yeah, it got a little crazy for a few moments," Dawson admitted.

"Is he gone?" Jason still looked frightened.

"As long as there's nothing else that belonged to him, you should be fine," Grady replied.

Pat and Jason came closer and shook hands with Grady and Dawson. "Thank you. I can't say that enough times," Pat said. "We had run out of options." He reached over and took Jason's hand. "What do we owe you?"

The Kings made a point of not charging for their services. They were the protectors of the mountain, a sacred responsibility. The auto body shops provided income. Hunting was a calling.

"Consider it a wedding present," Dawson said with a smile. "Best wishes, and all that jazz."

Pat and Jason stood arm in arm on the patio, waving as they backed out of the driveway and headed home.

"How are you, really?" Dawson asked, sparing a worried glance toward Grady, who was carefully rubbing his neck.

"Gonna be sore, but I'm okay otherwise." He managed a tired grin. "Just like old times, huh?"

"Yeah. It was." Dawson's heart held onto the hope that he and Grady could have what Pat and Jason had—a home, a shared dream, a forever love. "Felt good to kick some ass."

"Sure did," Grady agreed, as he closed his eyes and leaned back. "Wake me up when we get home."

Dawson glanced over often enough to assure himself Grady's breathing remained deep and even. Grady had held up his end of the fight better than Dawson had dared to expect. He knew that both of them were getting their feet back under themselves in so many ways, but he was willing to take success on the first hunt as a good sign.

This was more than he thought they might ever have, after his disastrous departure.

When Dawson had a few days' leave to visit before his deployment, Denny and Aaron hosted a picnic for all the neighbors and relations. Everyone greeted Dawson with backslaps and high fives, congratulating him on making it through Basic and wishing him well.

Grady hadn't shown up after the first hour, and Dawson feared he might not come, still smarting over the way they had left it months before. Then Grady came strolling in, holding hands with a good-looking stranger. Dawson focused on keeping his face impassive, even as his heart broke a bit more.

I told him to figure out what he wanted, Dawson reminded himself. *We didn't promise anything. If I was going to tie him to me, there was no point in going. I brought this on; now I've got to see it through.*

That didn't mean he had to like it.

Eventually, Grady and his new friend sauntered over. "Hiya, Dawson. Nice haircut."

"Hey, Grady. Good to see you."

"This is my boyfriend Ty. Ty—this is my cousin, Dawson."

Dawson didn't miss the way Grady emphasized the word "cousin," or the way he used Dawson's full name, something he rarely did. So this was a well-planned "fuck you." Dawson gritted his teeth and forced a smile.

"Nice to meet you. Hope you're hungry. There's lots of good food." Dawson intended to be polite if it killed him, and gauging from how much his heart hurt, it might.

"Oh, he's plenty hungry," Grady replied, meeting Dawson's gaze in a challenge, stressing that last word. Ty snickered. Apparently, Grady wanted paybacks. *The little shit.*

"Then you've come to the right place," Dawson said, unable to keep a chill out of his voice. He pretended to see someone over Grady's shoulder and waved in acknowledgment. "Gotta go."

For the rest of that awful afternoon, Dawson mingled with neighbors whose names he barely remembered and relatives he couldn't place on a family tree. He answered the same questions over and over about his plans for the military, his specialty, and whether he thought he might make a career of it.

All the while, Dawson remained aware of Grady's location, like a homing beacon. Out of the corner of his eye, he saw the two of them making a show of flirting and teasing each other. He caught a look of disapproval on Aaron's face. That sort of thing didn't go over well, no matter which genders were involved. Dawson saw a different look on Denny's face, one of pity and resignation. Dawson forced himself to look away.

I made my bed, and now I'll lie in it. Still think I did the right thing. But if I did, why does it hurt so fuckin' much?

———

Present Day

Dawson nosed the Mustang into its usual spot, and the rumble of its engine gentled to a purr as he shifted out of gear. Grady slept the whole way home, and Dawson couldn't help feeling guilty about putting him in danger when he saw the darkened bruises above the collar of Grady's T-shirt.

I thought getting back into a hunt would help him work through things. Maybe I made a mistake.

Then again, Grady had held his own against the ghost, doing Dawson proud. He'd gotten hurt, but they had both taken much worse injuries on hunts over the years, and it hadn't stopped them yet.

Trying to roll him up in bubble wrap isn't going to solve the problem. Although a mental picture of Grady, naked and wrapped in plastic gave him all kinds of ideas he really didn't need right now.

There's no rush, Dawson told himself for the millionth time, although his stiff dick didn't seem to be on board with that opinion. *He needs a friend right now more than a lover who doesn't have his own shit together.*

But as Dawson gazed at the sleeping man beside him, he wondered if he had the strength to wait.

Maybe it's good that we have that whole ridiculous "welcome home" reception this weekend, Dawson thought. *It's an excuse not to go right back out on another hunt, and it might be a nice change to do something fun. There are a lot of people I haven't seen yet since I've been back. And the fact that it'll give Sheriff Rollins indigestion? That's a bonus.*

6

GRADY

"If the phantom train's been around for seventy years, how come no one else in the family ever did anything about it?" Grady asked as he and Dawson sat in the front seat of the Mustang, staring out at a decommissioned railroad crossing on an abandoned road.

"Because it only happens every ten years. And at least the last three times the phantom train made its appearance, someone died."

"So, it's a harbinger?"

Dawson shook his head. "The people who died either happened to be at the crossing at the wrong time or had come out to look for the ghost train."

"You mean it kills legend trippers—like us."

"Uh-huh. Probably why Rollins promised not to give us a hard time about being here, after he made a big deal out of saying he'd arrest anyone who came out here looking for a thrill." Dawson made a sour face. "I imagine he figured he'd let the train get us out of his hair for good."

Today had been a good day, so far, with beautiful weather and bright sun. Grady'd only had one panic attack in the week since the B&B haunting, and while depression still nipped at his heels, and memories overwhelmed him from time to time, keeping busy helped. *Being with Dawson helped even more.*

Even though Dawson had yet to make any kind of move that might be considered "romantic," just being with him, like old times, healed a hole in Grady's soul.

Grady knew he couldn't rush the grieving process for his father, and that it would take time to let go of the lingering guilt. Dawson wasn't a hundred percent, either. Grady had heard Dawson cry out in the middle of the night more than once, a shout of fear and pain that chilled Grady to his bones. He'd been up and out of bed, padding toward Dawson's room before he even consciously thought about it, ready to protect and console.

Denny intercepted him, warning him off. Denny had told him that Dawson needed some time to adjust and that later on, Grady's help would be welcomed, but maybe not quite yet. Grady had been frustrated at not being able to ease Dawson's obvious distress, but he also took an odd sense of comfort from the meaning he chose to read into Denny's words, that later on, things between them would be different.

Grady hung onto whatever straws he could grasp since while Dawson had been relentlessly supportive, kind, and encouraging, he hadn't brought up their promise to each other in that last call before everything happened.

Seeing Dawson at the "welcome home" reception had made those memories burn brighter, fanning the embers of that familiar longing. Dawson fell back naturally into being a local, joking with family friends and neighbors, just like old times. He took the cake and parade and photographer in stride, sharing a few "put upon" smiles with Grady when no one was looking. Grady figured that seeing Sheriff Rollins fuming at the edge of the crowd just made everything that much sweeter for Dawson.

Grady had been beside him nearly the whole time, playing the same role he had back before Dawson left—best friend, sidekick, hunting partner. He'd gone along with it, happy to be at Dawson's side, although inside, he chafed at the description that was missing —"boyfriend."

Dawson had made sure Grady was included and made plenty of side comments and in-jokes when no one was looking. He seemed content to have Grady with him. But nothing he did really counted as flirting.

Then again, I haven't exactly been up to much flirting myself.

Still, he couldn't quiet all the worries. *It's really a miracle Dawson's even speaking to me after I was such a dick to him that first time he came home on leave.*

Out of all the things Grady wished he could do over, that awful picnic headed the list. He'd been hurting and angry about Dawson enlisting, especially since Dawson had told him in that last argument he was leaving—running away—to give Grady time to find himself. Or as Grady had taken it, to grow up. He'd felt rejected, abandoned, and heartbroken, and lashed out to give Dawson a taste.

They'd traded a few emails while Dawson was in training, mostly about the weather and local gossip. Nothing personal. Grady usually waited a few days before replying, partly to keep himself from saying things he might regret, and partly because he didn't want Dawson thinking he was waiting by the computer for a message.

Then Dawson had come home for a few days before he headed overseas, and Grady had pulled a real dick move, taking a guy he hardly knew to the picnic and practically making out with him in front of everyone, just to see if Dawson cared.

And as petty and wrong as it had been, Grady got what he thought he wanted. He saw the flash of hurt in Dawson's eyes, and the jealousy Dawson tried to hide. It had almost been worth the chewing out Grady had gotten from his father that night.

His triumph had been short-lived. Dawson had managed to be "busy" the whole next day, and then he was gone—for three and a half long years.

I thought we patched things up, in the years since then. I apologized. Daw said he forgave me. And there at the end, those last weeks before he was due to come home for good, he promised we'd try. But what if I misinterpreted it? Maybe Dawson's just giving me time to get back on my feet before he lets me down easy.

In his stronger moments, Grady knew anxiety fueled his fears. At other times, when shadows dogged his heels, those worries loomed large, and he couldn't quite remember the arguments he had used to talk himself down.

"What do you think is killing people?" Grady asked to pull himself out of his thoughts. They got out of the car and grabbed their gear bags from the back seat. "Another vengeful ghost?"

Since the last hunt went reasonably well, Grady was thrilled when Dawson brought up going out again. Dawson had come upon the situation while searching the internet in the wee hours of the morning when he hadn't been able to sleep.

"Denny thought it might be a little more complicated than that," Dawson replied, falling in step behind him. "Since a train isn't a living being, it shouldn't have a ghost. But the Nantahala Express was apparently cursed."

"A cursed, killer ghost train." Grady sighed. "This should be fun."

Dawson gave him a playful smack on the shoulder. "Of course it will be. Back in the saddle and all that."

Grady rolled his eyes, although he liked the way things were *almost* back to normal between them. The awkwardness had faded, and they fell into the same old jokes and teasing that had always been part of their relationship. *Except I don't want just normal. I want more.*

Grady squelched that thought, at least for now. They had a job to do. "We couldn't have just done a simple salt and burn, maybe dispelled a woman in white or a ghostly hitchhiker? We have to take on a whole friggin' phantom train?"

"Go big or go home," Dawson teased with a grin.

They headed toward the crossing, where the tracks cut through the asphalt of the roadbed. Weeds grew up through the gravel between the steel rails and over the rotting wood cross-ties. The road surface, untended for decades, showed its age with deep cracks.

Dawson set his bag down and put his hands on his hips, looking in one direction and then the other along the right of way that still remained clear for the old railroad line.

"The Nantahala Express mostly carried lumber, but it had a passenger car to bring workers out to the mill. Sometimes, the mill owners used it to get down through the mountains to where they could catch another train to one of the cities. Except according to what Denny and I could find, it all went really wrong one night."

Grady loved the lore and the stories around what they hunted as much as he did the thrill of the chase. The tales of how monsters and vengeful spirits came to be were as exciting as any superhero movie, and while regular people dismissed them as campfire stories, Grady knew that most held at least a grain of truth.

"I found an interview a small-town newspaper reporter did a long time ago with a guy who had worked at the lumber mill as a young man. The guy said he was there when the train made its last run." Dawson went on as he set out the items they were likely to need.

"There was a stand of trees the tribe that originally owned the land called a 'bad place.' No one was allowed to trap or hunt there, and people usually went out of their way to go around it. When the land was sold, the deed carved out that 'bad place' from being forested. It was supposed to be a preserve, forever."

"Wait, I think I saw this movie," Grady said, helping Dawson with the preparations. "The trees were so big that the mill owner decided to cut them anyhow, and things went downhill after that."

"And here I thought you fell asleep during all those late-night horror flicks we used to watch," Dawson joked. "Turns out you were paying attention after all."

"You'd be surprised at what I paid attention to," Grady quipped, then reddened and turned away as he realized how that sounded. He had promised himself he wouldn't flirt, wouldn't pressure Dawson. But after their short time hunting together again, Grady's dreams and fantasies had resurfaced and he'd been relieved to feel something other than guilt and grief.

"You might be surprised yourself," Dawson murmured, almost too quietly for Grady to hear. When Grady looked over, his partner busied himself with an old book and a silver bowl, assembling the ingredients for a ritual cleansing.

"Is that what caused the curse? Cutting the trees?" Grady asked as he chalked a sequence of sigils onto the asphalt, one of the things required to break the curse and free the spirit trapped inside the ghostly train.

"The legend said that the trees trapped a malicious nature spirit, and as long as the trees stood, the elemental would remain bound," Dawson replied. "If the trees were disturbed, those who caused them to fall and carried them away would be cursed. So the logs probably carried the spirit with them."

"Sounds likely."

"Then there's who happened to be on board. The mill owner had made a special trip to see the logs come in from that stand of trees. He was the one who personally ordered them to be cut, even though the foreman and the crew made it clear they didn't want to go near the place. The engineer and the conductor both had sketchy pasts— one barely escaped a murder conviction, and the other was said to have killed his wife in a drunken fury."

"You've got to be kidding me. This sounds like something straight out of a scream fest movie. All we're missing is a lonely summer camp, horny teenagers, and some creepy counselors," Grady protested.

"I can't make this stuff up." Dawson put a hand over his heart. "I swear, this is what the old guy told the reporter. You want to hear the rest or not?"

Grady gave an exaggerated sigh. "Go ahead."

"There was no one on the train that night except those three men and the cursed trees," Dawson went on. "The guy telling the story says he worked at the station in Highlands. He could see the sensors that told when a train passed certain points. And the Nantahala Express was flying. He tried to radio the engine room, but nobody answered. He says he thought for sure the train would jump the rails on a curve and crash. But when the train hit the flat land, it slowed down, and practically coasted into the Highlands station."

"Let me guess—everyone on board was dead."

"Got it in one," Dawson confirmed. "And they all looked as if they had died either in utter terror or that their hearts just...stopped."

"What about the cursed trees?"

"People were pretty freaked about what happened. Someone set the logs on fire, and witnesses said the flames burned green," Dawson replied. "No one was ever charged."

"And you think what we brought will stop an elemental spirit from doing whatever it damn well pleases?" Grady eyed the area around them suspiciously, in case the killer entity was listening.

Dawson nodded, with an expression of confidence Grady knew from long experience meant the other man was white-knuckling this with his best shot. "I think the approach is solid. It's gonna work."

"It better."

"It will."

"And the type of spirit has a name. It's an *Algos*. The ancient Greeks talked about them as the spirits of pain and misery—all the negative emotions. Sort of a psychic vampire. So we treat it like a vampire—with a little something extra thrown in."

Long before sunset, Dawson and Grady were ready. Grady had helped collect the items, and Dawson walked him through the plan again as they prepared the site.

"We've got to stop the phantom train, draw out the *Algos*, and then weaken it so it can be trapped in a spelled container."

"Please tell me the container doesn't go in the root cellar," Grady said. "Those old canned peaches down there are scary enough."

Dawson shook his head. "Denny knows where the cursed woods are located. He said he would take the spirit back there and bury the container. That sends it to its home and gets it out of our hair."

Together they had spread the contents of a large bag of rice across the rusted tracks since vampires—even psychic ones—were known to have an obsessive need to count spilled grains. That should force the *Algos* to stop the ghostly train and come out to deal with the rice. The protective sigils Grady had chalked on the road surface beneath the rice were an additional way to trap the spirit so they could use the array of weapons Dawson and Grady had brought with them.

They waited together near the lonely crossing as the sun dipped below the horizon. Wind rustled through the trees. The abandoned stretch of track and road were a long way from anywhere, and with the Mustang's headlights turned off, only moonlight broke the darkness.

"Listen."

Grady looked up at Dawson's whisper, and then he heard it, a mournful train whistle in the distance, on a track where no real engine had been in more than half a century.

"It's getting louder." Grady couldn't help it as a shiver ran through him. The sound seemed to reach deep inside and tangle around his darkest thoughts and feelings, pulling them to the fore as he fought to push them back.

Steel wheels scraped against the track, a rhythmic, hypnotic rumble. The ground beneath his feet trembled.

"There!" Grady pointed to the left, toward a pinprick of bright light that shouldn't exist. The light grew larger and brighter, and Grady's eyes widened as he realized that behind the train's headlight, he could see the massive form of a red diesel engine. The thunderous roar and the *clack-clack* of the wheels grew painfully loud, and when the whistle sounded again, it almost drove Grady to his knees.

"Get ready," Dawson warned. A dim bluish light glowed in the chalice where he had set a spell in motion, ready to be triggered at his word. Beside the chalice sat a silver bottle with runes and sigils marked in its sides, top open to receive the *Algos*.

Steel screeched against steel, throwing up sparks as the all-too-solid phantom train shuddered to a halt over the rice and sigils.

Grady felt like his heart might beat out of his chest as he gripped the Molotov cocktails made with blessed oil. Dawson froze, waiting for the right moment, with a specially-loaded shotgun in one hand and a unique grenade in the other.

For a few seconds, nothing happened. Then the door to the cab *wrinkled* more than opened, and a wraith-like, shadowy form emerged.

"Now!" Dawson yelled as the *Algos* found itself trapped by the rice and sigils.

Grady lit the wicks in his homemade bombs, and he lobbed them one after another. They landed at the wraith's feet, bursting into flame as the glass shattered, and the holy oil caught fire.

Dawson pumped round after round into the too-thin, gray shape. The rounds held not just iron and rock salt but also colloidal silver, deadly to vampires of any kind.

Before Dawson reloaded, he lobbed the UV grenade he had rigged, and it rolled to the feet of the *Algos*. "Fire in the hole!" he yelled.

Both Dawson and Grady threw their arms up to shield their eyes and clamp against their ears as the flash-bang went off. Even with his eyes closed and protected by his arm, Grady saw bright crimson through his eyelids at the burst of man-made daylight.

The *Algos* screamed, and the sound knifed through Grady. He dropped the bottle in his hand as his knees buckled, and he felt something reach into his mind and release all his grief and pain.

Dawson shouted his name, but Grady could not reply. All the heartache he had shuttered away, the guilt and blame, and the debilitating, bottomless black hole of depression that he had fought so hard to put behind him—all of it surged to the fore, overwhelming and suffocating him.

Nothing outside his own trembling body existed, as Grady struggled to keep from drowning in the flood tide of regret and recriminations. He fought against the surge that forced its way into his mind, feasting on his pain. Every mistake, every word said in anger, every failure boiled to the top, and Grady knew he couldn't fight forever.

It's true, all of it's true. I'm sorry. I'm so, so sorry...

An explosion broke through the bleak tide, and the power that had churned loose the muck of his soul receded. He heard a distant voice chanting an ancient language, and then a scream that felt like claws scraping down his bones.

Hands gripped his shoulders. "Gray? Come on, Gray, where are you? I got it. That damn *Algos* bitch is trapped. I didn't think she'd go after you. Oh, Christ, I should have realized. Please, Gray, wake up."

Grady heard the desperation and fear in Dawson's voice, but he felt too empty and harrowed to respond. He knew what they'd over-looked a second too late. The *Algos* fed on pain. Dawson hadn't believed Grady's guilt was deserved, so he hadn't factored that in as a weakness. Grady thought he had locked the worst away, started to deal with it. The *Algos* proved them both wrong.

Strong arms scooped him up, held him against a broad, warm chest. Grady could hear Dawson's shaky breathing, felt his pounding heart.

"I've got her trapped. She's in the lead box in the trunk. Gotta get you home. I'll call Denny on the way, tell him I fucked up. Jesus, Gray. I am so sorry."

Grady felt the leather of the Mustang's seat against his back as Dawson gently set him down. "I'll take care of you," Dawson promised, slamming the passenger door and going around to open the driver's side. The Mustang rumbled to life, and Dawson peeled out.

Grady floated between sleep and unconsciousness. Fragments of memories came to him, as if the dirt the *Algos* had churned up from the bottom of his soul had yet to settle.

———

Three Years Ago

He remembered emailing Dawson, drunk and sobbing, after he caught the boy he'd been dating cheating on him. The argument had been brutal—words said and punches thrown—and while Grady knew he hadn't been in love with the creep, he had tried, dammit. Tried to find out if anyone would ever capture his heart the way

Dawson had from the beginning. Tried to do what Dawson wanted him to do, to find someone else, and see if the feelings were any more real.

The attraction hadn't been. The pain was.

Grady had poured out his hurt and anger in a series of emails interrupted by puking up the Jack Daniels he'd swallowed as anesthetic. He hadn't even considered the time difference, that his day was Dawson's middle of the night. He hadn't stopped to think that Dawson probably didn't want to hear about his heartbreak. Or that maybe Dawson didn't want to hear from him at all.

He just knew that Dawson was who he needed, the destination his inner compass had always deemed to be true north.

Grady didn't remember what Dawson replied, only that it cheered him up, consoled him, told him to try again. He'd read and re-read the emails, searching for some hint that Dawson had changed his mind about where they left things, but found no hidden message.

He did care. That was stupid and selfish. I didn't mean to hurt him; God, I was flailing. But that didn't make it right.

After that, he and Dawson emailed more regularly. A few months later, Grady mentioned in passing that he was seeing someone else; Dawson wished him well. Mostly they talked about food and the weather, anything except the tension still between them.

There'd been another night, later on, when Grady had emailed Dawson to let him know the new boyfriend was history, and that Grady wasn't in the market anymore, that he was waiting for the right person.

Dawson consoled him, encouraged him, told him it would all work out. What he didn't do was promise anything, and that hurt far more than any breakup.

Dawson's news wasn't any better. He wouldn't be able to come home for a long while, and he wasn't likely to be able to email regularly. Grady knew that meant Dawson's unit was getting moved to somewhere in the thick of things. Grady had never been so afraid, terrified that he would lose Dawson before he had a chance to make things right...

———

PRESENT DAY

When he came around, Grady heard voices nearby.

"You aren't the only one who missed the part about feeding on guilt," Denny said raggedly. "Quit blaming yourself. Grady didn't pick up on it either, did he?"

Grady lacked the energy to open his eyes. He wondered how long he'd been out, and whether Denny and Dawson had been arguing the whole time.

"I should have," Dawson murmured, sounding close to where Grady lay. "I can't believe I practically served him up on a platter to a vampire that feeds on pain."

"Everyone's got pain and guilt and secrets," Denny argued. "It's the human condition. You think I can't hear you yell in the middle of the night? It could have just as easily gone after you."

"But it didn't."

"God, you are impossible. Fine. Beat yourself up. I've got a buggy whip in the barn if you want to do it right. Just don't be late for supper. I'm not keeping it warm for you." Denny shut the door a little too hard behind him.

Grady floated in comfortable darkness, unwilling to move, completely drained.

"I'm sorry," Dawson said quietly, sounding wrecked. "This is all my fault. Denny says you'll be okay, that you just need to rest. The *Algos* can't hurt you anymore; we took care of it. So just...sleep. I'll be here standing guard. We'll talk when you wake up."

For all the times in his life Grady had wished that he couldn't feel anything, now he realized how wrong he'd been. Whether the *Algos* had drained his emotions or exhaustion grayed everything out, the lack of strong feelings made him question if he was still alive.

He wanted to reassure Dawson, give some kind of signal. All he could manage was a twitch of his hand. Dawson's fingers closed around his, firm and strong.

"Gray? Can you hear me?"

Another twitch. Dawson sighed in relief.

"Good. That's good. The *Algos* fed on you, and it's going to leave you feeling pretty wrung out for a while, but it wasn't long enough to do permanent damage. So just rest. I'll be here. I promise."

Knowing he was safe, Grady stopped struggling and sank into a deep, dreamless sleep.

7

DAWSON

DAWSON WOKE, THEN GRIMACED AT HIS SORE NECK AND STIFF BACK. HE blinked, getting his bearings and realized he had spent the night in an armchair beside Grady's bed.

The memories rushed back, of the *Algos*, the phantom train, and Grady collapsing, refusing to wake. Guilt and worry washed over him. Dawson watched Grady's even breathing, felt for the pulse in his neck, and then allowed himself to relax.

He's okay. He's going to be okay.

As injuries went on a hunt, they had been lucky. No one came back bloody. That hadn't stopped Dawson's terror when he had seen Grady seizing as the *Algos* ransacked his worst memories and deepest fears.

Not all wounds bleed. I should have known better. Was this what the omen foretold? Did we cheat death? Or is there something worse, waiting for a shot?

He stared at Grady, wondering why everything kept going wrong. All he'd wanted was to come back home, make good on his promise to Grady, and start a new chapter of his life. Instead, the universe seemed to be conspiring against them.

Every time he thought Grady had started to heal, that the time might be right to bring up what they had promised, a new setback made Dawson cautious. They had to be equals in this, or it wouldn't work. That meant not pressing Grady to start something when he was vulnerable. Dawson hadn't waited this long just to fuck it up now.

Denny had gotten Grady to swallow a sleeping pill, and the low snores told Dawson the pill hadn't worn off yet. At least Grady hadn't woken screaming. Maybe, in a weird way, the *Algos's* attack might make all those difficult emotions a bit easier to process by tempering them so that they filtered back a little at a time. The lore Dawson had read suggested that as long as the *Algos's* feeding was interrupted short of death, the memories of the troubling emotions would gradually return. Dawson knew Grady wouldn't want to forget his father's death, but he didn't need to be overwhelmed with it, either.

"I'm here," he said quietly, rubbing his eyes. Dawson's dreams had been troubled, first by reliving the incident with the phantom train— only with different endings, none of them good. Then he'd seen the Black Shuck for the second time since Aaron's death. The dreams changed and he was back on base, remembering other things he'd rather leave forgotten.

Two Years Ago

Dawson had no one to blame but himself. He'd been the one who ran away to the military, the one to tell Grady that he needed to "find himself," the one to resist what Grady shamelessly offered him, what he desperately wanted.

So when Grady had shown up at that picnic with a creeper boyfriend, Dawson told himself this was part of the process. When Grady emailed him in the middle of the night, distraught over a breakup with a new guy Dawson hadn't even known about, Dawson bit his lip until it bled, clenched his fists until his nails dug into his palms, and provided as much comfort and insight as he could manage in a typed reply.

Dawson had seen enough pictures of happy same-sex military couples to know that finding love wasn't impossible, even though the Army talked a better game than it walked. But Dawson also knew he wasn't military for life, and his self-imposed exile hadn't been because he needed clarity. He already knew where his heart lay.

When the need for company finally overwhelmed him, Dawson could usually find a bar where he could get relief, no strings attached. Just like those last desperate months before he left home, he didn't fool himself about the type of guy he gravitated toward. They all looked like Grady, same hair, same build. If he kept his eyes shut, didn't look at the face, Dawson could pretend he was with Grady, with more realism than his solo jerk-off sessions.

He and Grady emailed a little more often than before. When another new boyfriend didn't pan out, and Grady said he was holding out for the right one, Dawson's heart stuttered in hope. After that, their conversation flowed better as they talked about everything and anything, and Dawson felt closer to Grady than ever before.

Not only that, but the tone of Grady's comments shifted over time as he talked about community college, hunting with his father, and everyday life. He'd started to come into his own, more confident and increasingly his own man. That was everything Dawson had hoped would happen. When he got home, he'd be twenty-three, and Grady would be twenty-one. Hardly old, but hopefully more mature than the teenagers they had been. Now, all he had to do was finish up his tour and see what they could make of their second chance. He only had one more year to go.

He dreamed again of the Black Shuck, the first time in a long while, since before his parents' death. This time, the beast chased hard on his heels, red eyes gleaming. Dawson woke in a cold sweat, knowing the vision was a true omen.

The urgency of the vision stayed with Dawson as they got ready to head out on a convoy. He knew there was no way to warn anyone without sounding crazy. Even his commander didn't have the authority to delay or reroute the mission.

The most Dawson could affect was his team's Jeep, and he did his best to get the guys on his team to sit on the side of the Jeep that would ride against the inside of the mountain roads, next to the cliff. They put the supplies on the outward side. He hoped it would make a difference.

Then everything went horribly wrong. Dawson remembered a deafening roar, gunfire, and the smell of blood, along with agonizing pain.

The first time he came to, pain nearly dragged him under. He heard medics barking instructions, then the pinch of a needle, and a blessed warmth swam through his veins.

He surfaced again, and it hurt to breathe. Monitors beeped, someone hurried closer, blocking his view, and then another pinch before he went under again.

Once he thought he remembered waking, but his skin burned with fever, his eyes hurt, and his whole body throbbed. Dawson heard worried voices, but he couldn't make out their words. Everything faded to gray.

"Do you know where you are, son?" the doctor asked when Dawson finally fought his way out of the darkness.

"We were under fire…"

The older man nodded. "Your convoy was ambushed. That's how you ended up with a bullet and some shrapnel in your ribs."

That fit with the patchy memories trying to surface. Men screaming in agony while others shouted curses and obscenities at their attackers. The stench of burning gasoline. The strange sound when he tried to draw a breath, and the awful pain that went with it.

"What about the others?"

"Most of them didn't make it. The lead Jeep hit an IED, and the snipers were waiting to pick off the rest of you. The only way anyone got out of there was because one of our choppers happened to be close enough to see the explosion and chased off the attackers."

The doctor paused, and looked like he wanted to ask a question, then thought better of it. "Your Jeep had fewer casualties than the others. I don't know what possessed your men to sit on the side toward the inside cliff wall, but it's the reason the ones who survived are still here."

The Black Shuck had been a harbinger, and its prediction proved true. Dawson knew he couldn't have prevented the mission, but he still felt responsible for the deaths, even though his last-minute shuffle had made a small difference.

"How bad am I?"

"The bullet broke a rib and punctured a lung. The piece of shrapnel didn't hit anything vital, but it tore you up pretty bad. You lost a lot of blood before we could get you to the hospital. It was touch and go for a while." The doctor paused. "An infection set in, and that was almost worse than the original injuries. You're a lucky man."

"How long has it been?"

"Almost two weeks."

"My family—"

"They were notified that you were injured in the line of duty. We don't give updates until the situation resolves—one way or the other."

"Now what?" Dawson tried to process everything the doctor said. But the real question was—do I get to go home?

"You've made good progress. There's no reason you can't return to duty once you've fully recovered."

When they'd finally let him out of the hospital, Dawson was glad, for once, not to have the ability to do a video call. He'd lost weight, and he looked gaunt even to his own eyes. There was a lot he couldn't tell Grady and Denny, but he needed to make sure they knew he was alive.

His email had gotten an immediate response.

"*Thank God. We've been worried. You take care, and keep your head down,*" Denny replied, but Dawson didn't need to hear his voice to know how much the older man wasn't saying, how much he downplayed their concern.

"*Oh, my God! We've been scared to death. How bad is it? Are you okay? Does this mean you'll be coming home?*" Grady's relief warmed Dawson, making him more sure than ever that he knew where his heart lay.

He'd had time to think in the hospital, those moments between the fever spikes and the pain when he'd been lucid. Any doubts he ever had about Grady being the one for him burned away in the clarity brought by almost dying.

After that, he and Grady emailed every day when Dawson had signal and the safety to connect. Video calls were harder to arrange, but Grady stayed up all hours to make it work. Dawson had every reason to believe communications were monitored, so there was a lot they couldn't say, but they'd known each other long enough to be able to string together in-jokes, punchlines, memories, and quotes in a kind of personal code.

When Grady finally asked if their "deal" was still on, Dawson promised him that it was and that he wanted it very much. Grady casually mentioned that he hadn't seen anyone since that last breakup, and Dawson let him know that the same held true for him. He hadn't had any desire for the hookups since before his injury. And now that the days of his tour were finally winding down, Dawson couldn't wait to come home and make good on that promise. Except he hadn't known yet about Aaron's death and Grady's remorse over it.

———

Present Day

"You look like you need this coffee even more than I thought."

Uncle Denny's voice snapped Dawson out of his memories. He looked up to see the other man holding out a large mug, which Dawson accepted gratefully.

"Any change?" Denny's gaze swept over Grady, taking in details with a practiced eye.

Dawson shook his head. "He hasn't woken up yet."

"He will. I went back to those lore books we found, put in a call to a guy down in Myrtle Beach who knows more about this kind of thing than I do. Everything says that assuming the *Algos* doesn't actually kill the person, it just takes them a while to get their mojo back."

Dawson slipped his hand closer and wrapped his fingers around

Grady's wrist, silently telling him he was not alone. "I hope you're right. Seeing him like this—" Dawson turned away and blinked back tears. "I wish that damn vamp had gone for me, instead."

"How do you think we felt when you got yourself shot overseas?" Denny demanded. "They told us just enough to scare the hell out of us, then said they couldn't disclose any other details. I barely talked Grady out of doing a scrying spell—and only because I promised that I'd do it with him if we didn't hear anything by a certain time."

"Oh yeah?" No one had told him about that.

"Yeah. So give him time. He's had a rough month." Denny looked at the sleeping man again. "I've got soup made, for when he wakes up. He'll probably need to eat a lot to get his strength up. I grilled burgers, too. Just finished mine. If you want to eat yours, it's on the table."

Dawson shook his head. "Thanks but, I think I'll just bring it in here if that's okay."

Denny's expression softened. "I'll get it for you. Then try to get some sleep yourself."

"I slept," Dawson said with a touch of defensiveness.

"Sleep more," Denny said, rolling his eyes. "I'll be right back."

Dawson choked down the burger, but nothing tasted good, and his stomach nearly rebelled. He felt certain he wouldn't have an appetite until Grady woke up. The rest of the evening passed as he watched videos on his phone until he heard a groan in the bed next to him.

"Gray?" Dawson dropped his phone into his lap and turned to reach for Grady's arm.

"Daw?" Grady's voice, weak as it sounded, was still the best thing Dawson had heard.

"You're home. No permanent damage, although you scared the shit out of me and gave Denny a bad turn, too. But you're okay—just wiped out."

"Did we get it? The psi-vamp?"

Grady struggled to stay awake. But he seemed to remember how he got hurt, which meant the *Algos's* attack hadn't damaged his memories.

"Yeah. It's all taken care of. And I'm fine—except for having a heart attack waiting for your lazy ass to wake up." Dawson's tone softened at that last part. "Can you eat a little soup? You've got to be hungry."

"Sleep."

"If I help you sit up, will you try to eat a little bit?" Dawson coaxed.

Grady nodded, and Dawson gave a shout to Denny, who showed up minutes later with a warm bowl of chicken broth. He thought Grady might not accept his help to sit, but to his surprise, Grady leaned into him, as if he needed the contact as much as the food.

Halfway through the broth, Grady's eyes struggled to stay open. "Done," he murmured.

Dawson took the bowl away and set it on the nightstand, then eased Grady back down. "You need anything else?"

A flush crept up Grady's face, and Dawson couldn't help chuckling. "Do you need to take a leak?"

Grady nodded, pointedly not making eye contact.

"Okay, we can do this. You want me to walk you down the hall to the bathroom, or bring you a bucket?"

Grady gave him a murderous look, and Dawson raised his hands in appeasement. "Hey, just giving you options. Bathroom it is."

Dawson helped Grady sit on the side of the bed, then got a shoulder under him to support his weight. "I've got you." Dawson worried that he was doing most of the work to keep Grady on his feet. "Come on—one step at a time."

They shuffled down the hall. Dawson kept an arm around Grady's waist, hip to hip, with Grady's arm across his shoulders. When they reached the bathroom, Dawson opened the door and helped Grady hobble inside.

"I'm good," Grady said, still keeping his gaze averted.

"You sure?" Dawson doubted that, but he knew Grady wanted to preserve his dignity.

"Yeah." Grady put one hand on the sink to brace himself. Dawson tentatively eased his grip, and Grady almost plummeted through his arms.

"Whoa!" Dawson caught Grady and hauled him up. "Let's try that again."

"Fuck," Grady muttered.

"It's okay." Dawson tried to sound matter-of-fact. He and Grady had gone skinny dipping at the quarry as kids, taken showers in the rigged-up stall out back when they were too filthy to come inside, and stayed in enough motels on the road that it wasn't like he'd never seen Grady's dick.

But he hadn't been paying attention back then, hadn't decided he was in love, wasn't on the verge of starting a sexual relationship with the man. That changed everything.

"Let's get your pants down. Then I'll steady you, and you can do the honors," Dawson said. "I promise I won't look." *I really will try to keep that promise, but I remember noticing that he had a pretty nice package.*

"Sorry."

"Hey, it's no big deal." Dawson hoped Grady didn't notice how his hand shook while he loosened the drawstring of Grady's sweatpants. *Thank heaven they're not button-down jeans.*

Dawson pushed Grady's sweats and boxer-briefs down, managing to keep his promise by working from behind. That didn't stop him from appreciating Grady's fine ass. *More material for the spank bank. And maybe, before too long, more than just daydreams.*

"Um, can we get a little closer?" Grady sounded mortified. Dawson shuffled them closer, then hummed loudly while Grady pissed like a racehorse.

"Okay, I'm done," Grady said when he finished as if the humming had covered the sound.

"Hold on." Dawson ducked down to grab the briefs and sweats that were around Grady's ankles, which put him on eye level with that delicious ass. As much as he wanted to take a bite, he gritted his teeth and made it back to standing. Once he'd tied the drawstring and gotten Grady to the sink to wash up, they slowly made their way back to the bed.

Grady looked wrung out. Dawson helped him pivot to lie down again and get comfortable.

"Thanks," Grady still wouldn't meet his gaze.

"Happens to everyone," Dawson replied, wondering if the issue wasn't so much Dawson getting a peek as it was Grady's attraction to him. "Get some sleep, and I'll let you know when dinner's ready."

Grady nodded and fell asleep in minutes. Dawson shifted in the armchair and pulled out his e-reader, bored with videos and games, and tried to finish the spy novel he had started the night before.

He woke with a start when Denny came in, realizing several hours had passed.

"Here," Denny said, carrying a footstool with one hand and a glass of whiskey in the other. "Figured you'd need these if you're going to sleep in here again." He set down the stool and handed off the glass. "How's he doing?"

"Not a peep after we got back from the bathroom. I got some of the soup into him."

Denny walked over and picked up the bowl from lunch. "It's a start. Once he wakes up again, I don't imagine he'll be very patient. If you two ever had a bucket list of one-day road trips, now might be a good time. I don't think he'll be up to hunting for a couple of weeks."

"I can come up with something. There should be enough roadside attractions and awesome diners to keep us busy." Dawson sobered. "What about work? Won't the shop be expecting us?"

Denny rolled his eyes. "Can't hardly send him in when he can't stand up, now can I? And he needs you here with him. But seeing how you're both part-owners, I imagine we can figure something out."

"Thanks," Dawson replied, glancing worriedly at Grady. He reached over to pull up the blankets and tucked them gently around the sleeping man.

"I know this whole homecoming isn't going quite the way you planned."

Dawson shook his head. Denny had been his sounding board

throughout his tour of duty, even though his uncle hadn't been shy about letting Dawson know what he thought of his original enlistment.

"That's...an understatement. Guess it doesn't matter if we end up in the right place, but it's hard."

Denny clapped a hand on his shoulder. "You'll figure it out. Just give it time." He closed the door when he left.

Dawson got comfortable in the chair and pulled the blanket over himself before reaching for his whiskey and his book. Maybe Grady didn't actually need a bodyguard. But until he was good as new, Dawson intended to keep watch anyhow, just in case.

———

"I THINK I FOUND A HUNT," GRADY CALLED FROM THE NEXT ROOM.

Two weeks had passed since the phantom train incident. As Denny's research had predicted, Grady's strength returned, and his nightmares seemed to have retreated, at least for now. Dawson made good on his word to keep them both busy playing hometown tourists, which turned out to be more fun than either man expected. Best of all, they'd had plenty of time to spend in the Mustang on the open road, having the kind of conversations that only happened in a car on a long drive.

They had finally recaptured the camaraderie from before things became fraught, a side effect for which Dawson was grateful. He had intentionally not gone looking for any signs of supernatural trouble because he didn't want to push Grady into anything—romantically or hunting-wise—before he was ready.

"Oh yeah?" Dawson looked up as Grady padded out to the kitchen, barefoot. Faded jeans clung in all the right places, and the dark T-shirt fit snugly over defined muscles. Dawson pulled his attention back to his coffee and discreetly adjusted himself.

"Ghost lights."

Dawson sat back in his chair. "Like the Brown Mountain Lights? They're a long way from here." Unexplained, ghostly bobbing lights were a well-known phenomenon, but the mountain from which they took their name wasn't close. Although they'd been called in to help other hunters from time to time, the Kings generally had their hands full just dealing with the supernatural problems in Transylvania County and the western end of the state.

"Sort of, but not." Grady poured himself a cup of coffee, snagged a muffin off the plate on the counter, and sat across from Dawson. "They're newer, for one thing. Reports only date back about two months. Mostly, they've been a curiosity or a nuisance. Drivers complained that the lights popped out of nowhere and danced around, almost causing a wreck."

"Doesn't exactly sound like a hunt," Dawson replied. "Might be something natural, like foxfire. Or a plague of lightning bugs."

"I wondered about that, but then two hikers have gone missing in that same area, just since the ghost lights showed up."

"Did you ask if Denny knew anything about it?" Dawson feigned interest, but his mind spun, trying to figure out whether Grady was up to a hunt, even an easy one. Grady had some rough days right after the fight with the psi-vamp, and as he regained his strength, Dawson knew that the painful memories the *Algos* had fed from roared back with a vengeance.

Grady had nightmares—no, night terrors, Dawson corrected himself—several evenings in a row that left him pale, shaking, and throwing up. The dreams had become less frequent, with none at all in the past few days, but Dawson didn't want to add fuel to the fire. Even easy hunts could go badly wrong.

"He said it wouldn't hurt to check into it. I mean, it might just be a coincidence that the hikers disappeared after the lights showed up. But what if it isn't?"

"Where is it?"

"Over on Wolf Mountain. I already checked—it'll take us about an hour to get there. I already have the coordinates for the trail the hikers were on, and the location of the roads where the ghost lights showed up. And if it all is a bust, there's also a hometown barbecue place nearby that gets rave reviews."

Grady's pitch was smooth enough that Dawson wondered how many time's he'd practiced. But he couldn't ignore the excitement in Grady's eyes, after weeks when he thought he might never see that light again.

Still, he didn't want to give in too easily. "Well, okay," he said with an exaggerated sigh. "But only for the barbecue."

"Yes!" Grady did a fist pump, and Dawson raised an eyebrow.

"Seriously? I know you don't have cabin fever. We put a couple hundred miles on Sally just joyriding."

Grady's smile slipped a little, and Dawson immediately regretted his words. "It sounds like an easy hunt—as easy as they ever are. I need to get back in the saddle, Daw. The last one didn't end well, and I need to prove to myself I'm not afraid."

"Okay, then. Should have said so in the beginning. I'll grab some muffins for the road and throw some soda in the cooler, and you can let Denny know where we're going."

"Already did."

Dawson laughed. "So pitching me, that was just for show?"

"Pretty much, yeah."

Dawson grinned. That was the sassy, feisty side of Grady he'd barely glimpsed since he'd come home, the side he feared might have died along with Aaron and the werewolf. "If that's the case, then you grab the muffins, I'll get the gear bag, and let's hit the road."

The cool, sunny day seemed tailor-made for a drive. Wind rustled the tops of the trees, sending shifting shadows across the asphalt. Dawson turned up the music and rolled down his window.

Grady hadn't said much about the most recent nightmares, only that they were more of the same. Dawson hadn't pressed because he figured they were aftershocks from the *Algos's* attack as Grady's savaged memories reintegrated. He'd hoped at first that the psi-vamp might have taken the painful images away permanently, then realized that wasn't fair to Grady. His memories, no matter how awful, were part of who he was and shaped his choices, just as Dawson's own dark remembrances did.

That didn't mean he was happy about seeing Grady relive his pain.

Dawson wasn't about to ask and ruin the mood, but he worried about his companion's sudden cheer. *What's wrong with me? I worry when he's sad. Then I worry when he's happy. What's he supposed to be?*

Maybe it was nothing. Dawson certainly tried to talk himself out of his concern. He knew his own PTSD made him hyper-vigilant, and Grady's close call just ramped Dawson's usual protectiveness into overdrive.

Still, he survived in the Army and as a hunter by listening to his gut, and if his intuition said he needed to keep a close eye on Grady, then Dawson would do just that.

"Did we ever hunt anything out here?" Dawson asked.

After a while, it got difficult to remember where all they'd been, especially since while they were growing up, their fathers, cousins, aunts, and uncles had also been active hunting, and they had heard about it afterward.

"It sounded familiar to me too, but I don't remember being there," Grady agreed. "Maybe we heard a story from someone."

"Yeah, that must be it." Denny had a logbook of all the places the family had hunted that went back a couple of decades. Dawson realized that he should have stopped to check, but since the log was on paper and not the computer, that would have meant hours scanning entries, and Grady had been champing at the bit.

"Hit me with the details—we've got time," Dawson said after they'd gotten a good start. He turned down the music and rolled his window up so he could concentrate on what Grady had to say.

"Pretty skimpy, really. The lights showed up out on Long Branch Road two months ago. People who've seen them say the lights attacked them."

"Attacked?"

Grady nodded. "Dove at them. Dive-bombed them. Didn't hurt anyone directly or break anything, but one of the drivers said the lights seemed to be 'playing chicken' with his car—his words, not mine."

That almost sounded sentient. "Please tell me there aren't legends about the Fey on Wolf Mountain."

Grady frowned. "Not that I've seen."

"There's a reason some places call mysterious glowy things 'fairy lights,'" Dawson replied. "And a lot of stories about the Fey showing up as will-o-the-wisps. We do not want to fuck with the Fey. If we see any mushroom circles, we're out of there. Denny knows how to make a peace offering. We stay the hell out of that shit."

"Works for me."

"Anything unusual about the people who went missing?"

Grady checked the notes on his phone. "Both were young and fit, experienced hikers, and local—so they knew the area."

"Anyone else go missing lately?"

Grady studied his research and frowned. "Huh. There another person who vanished near there a month before the two hikers or the lights. I didn't pick up on it before because he wasn't hiking. The report says no one was sure why he went into the woods. His car was pulled off to the side of the road, and he just walked into the underbrush. He didn't appear to have taken any equipment, nothing but the clothes he was wearing."

"Maybe he had to take a leak."

"That's honestly what someone suggested. But who walks into the woods to take a piss far enough to get lost?"

"And other than the one guy's car, they never found anything? Clothing, cell phones, body parts?" Something about this whole thing felt off to Dawson, but he still couldn't put his finger on the reason.

Grady shook his head. "Not that I could see in the reports. And before you ask, these were people who had a reason to come back. They had jobs, lovers, families, pets—they didn't wander off to end it all."

"Not sure whether that narrows anything down or not."

"Sure it does. It means they didn't go out there not wanting to be found. Whatever happened was either an accident or someone— some*thing*—got to them," Grady countered.

Dawson drove up and down Long Branch Road without incident. "Did the reports say the lights showed up at a particular time of day?"

"Just before sunset and into the evening," Grady replied. "I wouldn't expect this road to get a lot of nighttime traffic. There are a few houses and cabins out here, but from what I could tell, the road is mostly a way to reach trailhead parking lots."

"Where did the guy with the car disappear?"

Grady watched the landmarks until they came to the right place. "Here."

Dawson slowed the car, but as they peered out the windows, nothing exceptional struck them about the forest on either side of the road. "There's not even a trail," Dawson said. "Although the ground's pretty flat, so it wouldn't be hard to just walk into the woods. But why would anyone do that?"

He looked to Grady. "Is there anything unusual about the people who went missing? Weird jobs? Anything they had in common?"

Grady glanced through his notes again. "I couldn't find anything to connect them, except where they went missing. One of the hikers worked at a video game store. The other was a college student. They didn't know each other, and they weren't hiking together. The only thing I thought was interesting is that the car guy who just wandered off posted a lot to a Bigfoot-tracking blog."

"Bigfoot. Like the big hairy dude?"

"Yeah. He posted a lot of questions about how he wanted to be the one to find Bigfoot and prove it," Grady replied.

"So you think maybe he saw something strange and chased it?"

"Do you have a better theory?"

Dawson shook his head. "No. But since we don't know where the Bigfoot-chaser actually went, let's come back to him. We can start with the trails and see what we find."

They stopped for lunch at the barbecue place Grady found online. It lived up to its reputation, and Dawson decided to pick up some take-out for Denny on their way home. Grady seemed to be enjoying himself, and Dawson wondered whether part of that was because he had been the one who found the hunt and the restaurant.

If he wants to take the lead, it's fine with me, if that makes him feel more in control. I don't have to be in charge. That insight reminded Dawson that Grady hadn't been the only one who did some growing up in the years they were apart. He'd had his priorities shaken up by his near-miss, and the stripped-down military lifestyle had taught him a lot about essentials.

Dawson found a pull-off at the trail head and parked the Mustang far enough onto the berm to avoid getting sideswiped. He grabbed the gear bag filled with their weapons, salt, ammo, and emergency supplies. After their long-ago run-in with the wendigo, Dawson never risked going into the woods unprepared.

Grady had their trail maps marked, and they set off. The bright sunlight filtered through the leaves, and a light wind rustled the branches. They rarely had the chance to hike for pleasure when they didn't need to be on the alert for danger. Dawson added that to his mental bucket list for something to do as a date when they got to that stage.

"Neither of the trails the hikers were on had been marked dangerous or strenuous," Grady said. "They don't have caution notices or hazards like steep drop-offs nearby. None of the comments on the forestry website indicated that anyone had any problems— before the hikers vanished."

"We're missing something," Dawson fretted. "There's a piece we aren't seeing."

They had walked for half an hour before Grady stopped. "Do you hear that?"

"Hear what?"

"Exactly," Grady replied. "Where are the birds and the animals? Have you even seen a squirrel since we got on the trail? We should be spooking out rabbits and deer and chipmunks from cover, or see deer in the underbrush. The birds are usually loud. Where are they?"

Grady's question made the hair on the back of Dawson's neck rise. "Something's frightened them away—or eaten them." Bear and bobcats were two "normal" possibilities, along with a very long list of supernatural ones.

"That's my bet."

Shit. This was supposed to be a simple hunt for strange lights. Not dangerous. Fuck, we need to get out of here. They had brought weapons as a matter of course, but without knowing what they were hunting, they couldn't be sure that they had the right tools for the job. So many supernatural threats required unique, arcane defenses, and items unlikely to be readily on hand. Which meant that if they confronted whatever scared away the wildlife, odds were good that they might not be able to stop it or hold it off.

"Alright, let's go," Dawson said. "We don't know what we're up against, and I'm not in the mood to get my ass kicked."

"We just got here."

"It's not like we had to pay for a ticket," Dawson replied. "We can come back. Besides, we don't want to be in the woods after dark without a clue about what's out here with us."

"Daw, we're out in the dark with monsters all the time. It's kinda what we do."

"Maybe we should re-think that."

Underneath the trees, the afternoon sun already cast long shadows. Dawson's gut went from tense at the possibility of trouble to shouting for them to get the fuck out now.

"Daw—look."

Dawson turned to see two bobbing lights hovering eye-level over the trail. He moved to one side, as if to go around them, and they moved with him, blocking his way.

"Those aren't will-o-the-wisps. They're orbs. I think we found the missing hikers." Ghosts often manifested as glowing balls of light. "We just didn't connect the dots since people reported seeing them on the road."

"They don't want us to go on."

"Maybe it's a warning. Maybe that's why they 'attacked' the cars. We need to go."

"I think you're right."

Dawson pulled their shotguns from the pack and handed one to Grady. They turned around, heading out faster than they had hiked in. The orbs hovered a distance behind them but did not try to interact or stop them.

Out of the corner of his eye, Dawson caught a glimpse of motion, but when he turned, there was nothing. Clouds now filled the sky, dimming the sunlight. Dawson saw movement again, a shadow where a shadow shouldn't be...

"Watch out!" Grady yelled as a blur of hard muscle and black hair lunged from a cleft in the rock. Grady threw himself into Dawson, knocking him out of the way. The creature landed on Grady and took them both to the ground, rolling them over and over. Two glowing orbs dive-bombed the beast, trying to distract it from its prey.

"Shoot!" Grady yelled. Dawson brought up his shotgun, trying to get a clean shot. The salt, iron, and silver rounds would damage most supernatural beasts, but he needed to hit the monster, not Grady.

He couldn't get a good look at what had attacked them, except that it was almost as large as Grady, covered in fur and powerfully built. Grady struggled and fought, but the creature kept rolling them, and Dawson feared waiting for a shot would get Grady killed.

"Fuck you!" Dawson roared, drawing a silver-edged hunting knife from its belt sheath and charging toward the fray. He jumped on top of the monster and brought his knife down through its back, where the heart should be. The orbs kept up their silent assault, trying to come between Grady and the beast.

The thing reared back with a piercing shriek. Dawson tightened his legs around it like a bucking bronco and grabbed a fistful of coarse, matted fur with his left hand, drawing his blade across the throat in one clean movement.

It fell to one side, and Dawson rode it down, unwilling to risk having it flip over and gut him with its claws. Only when it stilled and stopped breathing did he finally release his grip. For good measure, he dropped the knife, grabbed the gun, and pumped a round into the creature's skull, just in case.

"Gray?" Dawson got to his knees and saw his partner lying in the middle of the trail, covered in blood.

"No, no, no!" Dawson scrambled over as Grady stirred. "Did it bite you? Are you hurt? Talk to me!" His heart thudded from the fight, and fear for Grady's safety sent adrenaline surging. So much blood covered both of them, and in the dim light, Dawson couldn't see whether Grady had been injured.

"Didn't get bitten," Grady managed, staring back at Dawson. "Did you?"

Dawson shook his head. He'd have bruises and sore muscles, but he'd been on the wrong side of the creature for it to reach him with either teeth or claws.

"Let me check you over." Dawson pulled a flashlight from his jacket and examined Grady for open wounds. Relief flooded through him when he didn't find any serious injuries.

"What was it?" Grady couldn't hide the way his voice shook. Dawson winced, thinking that the attack had to feel like one of Grady's nightmares, maybe like reliving the night Aaron died.

Dawson kicked at the dead creature, rolling it onto its back. He let out the breath he'd been holding when he recognized the form. It resembled a big wolf, but the proportions were different, the muzzle wrong, and its red eyes confirmed its supernatural nature.

Just like in the dream. Was it warning me about this attack? Or is there still more danger looking for us?

"Black Shuck. Not a werewolf, or a shifter. Just a Shuck." *Vicious fuckers, but no poison, and they don't turn you. Of course, seeing one in person is supposed to be worse luck than dreaming of them. Getting attacked by one is as bad luck as killing one.*

Dawson feared his nightmare omens had just gone from bad to worse.

The two orbs had quieted, hanging in mid-air like before. Dawson looked up at them. "You're the hikers. The Shuck killed you."

The orbs dipped and rose in unison. He took that as a "yes."

"You were trying to warn people, keep them away, weren't you?" Again, a dip and a rise confirmed his theory. "Could you lead us to your bodies if I came back tomorrow, so we can see to a decent burial?" This time, the lights moved side to side, a negative.

"No bodies?" Grady asked.

"Some creatures consume everything—bones and all," Dawson replied. "Do you need a priest?" Another side-to-side gave the answer. "Can you move on?"

The orbs dipped and rose one more time, and then flared brightly before vanishing.

Dawson sat down hard on his ass, feeling the aftermath of the fight and his fear for Grady. That's when realization hit.

"Tell me you weren't trying to get yourself killed."

Grady's eyes widened. "What? God, no! Why would you even say that?"

"Because you tackled that thing before we even knew what it was, like you didn't care if it got you."

Grady met his gaze defiantly, without backing down. "I knocked you out of the way."

"How did that help? You could have been killed!"

"Better me than you."

Dawson hauled Grady to his feet and held him by the front of his shirt. "Don't you say that. How in the hell would that be better?"

"I thought...I thought it was another werewolf. Like before. And I couldn't let it get you. I couldn't go through that again. Couldn't lose you, not like that. Not like that," he repeated. Grady's eyes were wide, but he didn't seem to be seeing Dawson in front of him. He had gone ashen, and his whole body trembled. Grady's breathing had grown shallow and fast, and a sheen of sweat beaded his forehead.

"Gray? Gray, it's alright. We're safe. The Shuck is dead." Dawson gripped Grady by the shoulders, fearing that the other man might fall if he let go. Then he pulled him into a bear hug with all his strength, trying to say with his body what he couldn't say in words.

"So much blood," Grady murmured when Dawson pulled back, as if he hadn't heard anything Dawson said. "Blood all over me, and the shot was so loud." He looked up, his expression bereft. "I can't get clean. Can't wash it off me. I can smell blood all the time."

Fuck, it's a full-blown panic attack. He's got this tangled up with what happened to Aaron. This is my fault. I shouldn't have yelled at him. But I was so fuckin' scared. So afraid that maybe he was looking for a way out—

"Gray? It's me, Daw. You're okay. I'm not hurt. No one is dead. The blood isn't ours. It was a Shuck, not a werewolf. Can you hear me? Do you understand? I'm not dead."

"Daw?" Grady seemed to be coming out of his fog.

"I'm here, Gray. We're safe."

"I heard the shot—"

"You and me, we're safe."

Grady licked his lips, not quite back to himself. The vulnerability in his expression made him look so young, Dawson thought and kicked himself for putting Grady in a situation that ripped the scabs off all the healing he had done.

Then again, if we'd known it was a Shuck, we wouldn't have taken the hunt, and let someone else have it. We thought it was just those stupid lights.

Knowing that didn't ease Dawson's guilt, not when he saw how terrified Grady had been.

"Couldn't lose you too. Couldn't see you die." The look in Grady's eyes held so much pain and loss that Dawson had to turn away. He pulled Grady to his chest, wrapping his arms around him again, and Grady slowly returned the hug.

"We're both alive, Gray. Can you hear my heart? We're okay." Grady clung to him for a couple of minutes before stepping back.

"Can you walk? We should get out of here." Dawson looked down at the Shuck's carcass. "We can leave that for the scavengers. I need to get you home."

He took in Grady's blood-soaked clothing, knowing that he looked just as bad. "Come on. I've got a change of clothing in the car for both of us."

Grady didn't speak as they walked back to the Mustang. His color had improved, at least as much as Dawson could tell in the fading light and beneath all that dried blood. The panic attack might have subsided, but Grady still looked rattled, and maybe a little embarrassed.

"Hey," Dawson said, bumping shoulders. "I get it. It's okay to be overwhelmed. Happens to everyone. I saw it a lot in the service."

"Doesn't happen to you."

"Mine usually sets in afterward," Dawson admitted. "You think I went off by myself after a bad hunt to meditate? Just didn't want you to see me get the shakes."

"Wouldn't have held it against you," Grady said in a small voice.

"I know that now. I know a lot of things now that I didn't know then."

Dawson didn't let down his guard on the walk back, especially since Grady wasn't quite himself yet. When they reached the Mustang, Dawson found the bag with their spare clothes in the trunk and a container of cleaning wipes.

"I can't do anything here about the blood in your hair, but this should help you get it off your face and hands." He held out the container to Grady. Dawson laid out clothing for the other man, keeping his attention on their surroundings to avoid any other surprises. Once Grady had finished, Dawson got him settled in the Mustang, then made short work of getting himself cleaned up and changed.

When he slipped behind the steering wheel, he looked over at Grady. His partner still looked shaken, eyes averted, and he slumped in the seat like something inside had broken.

Dawson reached over and gripped his shoulder. "You'll be alright. We'll be okay. It just takes time."

Grady nodded. Dawson started the car and headed for home. He'd skipped stopping for take-out BBQ for Denny, and figured he would make it up to his uncle. He turned on the radio, but kept the volume low, not sure whether a headache was part of Grady's reaction. Night had fallen, and the Mustang seemed to be alone on the road, its headlights the only light when clouds hid the moon.

"You really thought I was trying to check out?" Grady finally said, in a tone Dawson couldn't read.

"You scared me," Dawson replied, figuring he needed to lay his cards on the table. "You were on that thing before I saw it move, and I thought it was going to kill you. And I was afraid that maybe you were making some kind of atonement."

Grady stayed quiet so long Dawson feared he might not answer. *I need to know when to keep my big mouth shut. But he scared the living shit out of me.*

"I wasn't. I swear. But I knew if I had to see it happen all over again, I couldn't watch you die. And if it had been another werewolf, and you'd gotten bitten—I'd just rather it be me than you."

"Thank you for protecting me," Dawson said quietly. "But Gray—I feel the same way. If you'd been bitten, or hurt—" He couldn't finish.

"Are we okay?" Grady sounded so bereft; it was all Dawson could do not to pull the car over and wrap his arms around him again.

Why did all this have to happen before we had a chance to get our feet under us, together? It would be so much easier if we'd already crossed those lines. But if he's still this raw, he needs a best friend more than he needs a new lover. Just for a little while longer, until he's better.

"We're okay," Dawson confirmed. "Just gotta give yourself some more time to deal with everything."

"Thanks," Grady murmured.

Dawson nodded, although he wasn't exactly sure what Grady was thanking him for. "Why don't you get some sleep. I'm good to drive."

Grady turned toward the window, and Dawson knew from his breathing that he'd fallen asleep quickly. Thoughts churned as he drove through the night, none of them putting his mind at ease.

He believed that Grady told the truth about why he jumped the Shuck. But Dawson still had the feeling that the need for atonement, no matter how misguided, lurked just beneath the surface. Grady's mind might accept that what happened to Aaron wasn't his fault, but guilt and grief could become a tangled mess in the dark corners of the heart. Dawson knew that people often didn't truly understand why they did things until later. So if Grady's subconscious felt driven to punish him, hunting presented far too many opportunities for that to happen.

And then there were Dawson's visions of death omens, too many to discount. Either they'd been tremendously unlucky, or there was a bigger picture, a larger threat that Dawson didn't yet see. Regardless, he knew he had to keep Grady safe.

The more I try to protect him, the more he'll push back. Hell, I'd do the same in his shoes. So if he wants to hunt, we'll hunt. If I'm with him, maybe I can keep him safe. Despite everything, he did good today. His reflexes were sharp, and he didn't let the Shuck get in a bite. I've just got to keep my temper in check. Triggering one of those panic attacks isn't going to do anyone any good. I need to be his safe space. That's the only way we're going to get through this to the other side.

8

GRADY

"What the fuck happened?" Denny stared as Grady and Dawson walked in, hair matted with dried blood, streaks of it still on their skin where they'd missed spots with their hurried clean-up.

"Let Daw tell you." Grady dropped his bag just inside the door. "I need a shower—and a drink."

Grady heard them talking as he climbed the steps, but he didn't want to relive the night's events.

Even though he had changed clothing at the car, enough gore remained that the new shirt and pants still needed washing. He grabbed fresh clothes, then headed to the bathroom.

The hot water sluiced through his hair, washing away the remaining blood. Grady kept his eyes closed so he didn't see the runoff go down the drain. *Not human blood. Not Dad's, not Daw's. Hold it together.*

He tried breathing like he'd seen in a meditation video, counting to make himself focus. Next, he concentrated on the tight set of his shoulders, the clenching fists, and the tension running through his whole body coiled to respond. *Christ, I'm a mess.*

The smell of Irish Spring soap took away the stench of blood. As he lathered, he dug his fingers into the tense knots in his neck, shoulders, and jaw. He'd used one of those fancy massage chairs at a mall long ago and wished he had something like that handy.

If I could pull my head out of my ass, Daw could probably do a real good job with a massage...and maybe find other ways to blow off steam.

Just that morning, Grady had felt like his old self, sassy and alive. He'd watched Dawson's movements hungrily, perving unashamedly on the guy he remained certain was the love of his life. And this morning, Dawson flirted back.

He saw the interest in Dawson's eyes, noticed when he got hard in his jeans. Grady loved having that effect on Dawson, and he knew just how long they'd been dancing around each other. They had joked in the car as Grady recapped his research, and at lunch the cute waitress must have figured they were a couple because she didn't even make a half-hearted attempt to flirt with either of them.

The trail had been good too at first. Grady loved the outdoors, and the scenery in Transylvania County was some of the finest in the Blue Ridge and the whole of the Appalachians. Bright sun, breeze stirring in the trees, a pretty little waterfall—and Dawson beside him—had been even better than old times.

Then it all went to shit.

Grady scrubbed his hair again as if he could never get clean. His mind flashed an instant replay of the Black Shuck's attack, but the images were interspersed with ones from that awful night with the werewolf. The face he saw kept changing, sometimes it was Dawson's, and then it became his father's terrified expression.

He'd acted without needing to think, anything to protect Dawson, to keep from having to relive that awful choice, to hear that final gunshot. And then, when the Shuck's hot blood covered him, Grady was back *there*, that other forest trail, only it was his father's blood. So much blood.

Grady staggered from the shower, leaving it running, and barely made it to the toilet before he lost everything in his stomach. He got to his feet, turned off the water, and toweled himself dry, then did his best to sop up the water on the floor.

Dawson's accusation rang in his ears. Grady had been angry, defensive, and incredulous in response. Did Dawson really think he was that broken? *Am I?*

Grady knew he had lied to himself a time or two. Like right after Dawson left for the Army, when Grady'd been so angry he swore he never wanted to see him again; and he'd thrown himself into dating with a vengeance. It had taken months to admit to himself that the anger came from how much it hurt, and how having Dawson go off to the Army and leave him behind brought up all kinds of feelings connected to his mother's abandonment years before.

He'd believed himself when he denied Dawson's charge. And in his heart, Grady knew he couldn't have let Dawson get hurt, might not have survived seeing him get killed. If anything, Grady had more to live for now than ever before since Dawson was home, and they'd agreed to finally be boyfriends.

Except that one mess after another kept getting in the way. These past weeks certainly hadn't shown Grady at his best, and if he and Dawson hadn't known each other their entire lives, if he had just been an acquaintance, Grady knew he wouldn't have come off as boyfriend material.

Right now, he wasn't much good as a partner—in bed or on a hunt. Although he tried to put on a good face, his emotions had more dips and twists than a mega coaster at Carowinds. The nightmares had eased a bit, but he suspected today would provide fresh fodder. Dawson's dreams hadn't seemed as bad lately—at least, judging by how he hadn't woken them up screaming in a while—but that might change after today's clusterfuck.

Would it be any better if they were sleeping together, pressed close, holding tight, providing proof of life? At their age, even the apocalypse probably couldn't keep their dicks down for long. Could they fuck away the pain? And even if they could, was that what Grady wanted when he *finally* had Dawson in his bed?

Grady knew the answer. He wanted Dawson forever, not just to work off the hard edge after a hunt. He needed to deserve that love and be whole enough to return it. Right now, they were both a mess.

But damn, it frustrated the fuck out of him to have what he'd wanted so long almost in his grasp and still have to wait.

It could have been so much worse. Grady remembered the call that woke him in the middle of the night. He'd been groggy enough to hope it was somehow Dawson. Instead, it had been Denny.

———

TWO YEARS AGO

"Grady? Are you awake?"

The clock read three in the morning. No good phone calls ever happened after midnight.

"I am now." His mind cleared fast as fear took hold. "What's the matter? Did something happen to Daw?"

"We don't know all the details," Denny said, sounding strained. "Just got a call that said there had been an 'incident' and Dawson's been injured. The useless asshole who called me said he couldn't give me any other details. He told me they would be 'in touch,' but he didn't say when. Sorry to wake you, but I figured you'd want to know."

"Maybe they made a mistake," Grady said, clutching at straws. "The Army screws things up sometimes, right? Mistaken identity. Missing dog tags—"

"Pretty sure they didn't, not this time," Denny told him. "Too high tech these days. I imagine they'll tell us more when there's more to tell. I'll keep you posted."

Grady sat up, feeling as wired as if he'd downed a pot of coffee, and his gut clenched. "Thanks. I'm glad you told me. Just...if you hear anything—"

"Sure thing," Denny promised. "I thought about letting you sleep, but..." He didn't have to finish his sentence. Apparently, Denny didn't know how bad things were, or whether they might get unwelcome news sooner than expected.

"That's okay," Grady replied, although the situation was anything but. "Take care."

"You too."

The Kings had never been particularly devout. They'd hunted monsters in England throughout the religious wars, back in the day, and seen humans carry out monstrous atrocities in the name of God. Grady's father had always tried to be the epitome of a hunter to prove in his own mind that he was a real King. Aaron said that hunters needed to view the supernatural on its own terms, outside of dogma and superstition. That still never stopped hunters from calling out a prayer to anyone who might be listening when the going got rough.

Grady struggled to get himself under control. Dawson was half a world away. He'd never felt so helpless in his life.

What if Dawson didn't make it back? They'd only just begun patching up their relationship as best friends, only started rebuilding trust. Grady wanted so much more, and now he sensed that Dawson did too. But if Dawson died, far away from home, they'd never get the chance to see what they could become, and Grady would never know whether Dawson truly loved him.

Grady felt as if the bottom had dropped out of his world, and he had nothing solid to steady himself. He thumbed his phone open and pulled up his photos. So many over the years were of Dawson, some taken secretly, others crazy candids or just the two of them, horsing around. In all of them, Dawson stared back, eyes bright with mischief, and a wide smile that always made Grady's heart flip.

Grady knew he had to be up in a few hours for class, and he had a shift at the auto body shop after that. Work and class would keep him busy, but they couldn't push his worry out of mind. Nothing could. He sent up a plea to a god he wasn't sure he believed in, promising anything, everything, if only Dawson came home safe.

Days passed and no word came. Grady felt twitchy, like he'd had far too much caffeine, noticeable enough that his classmates asked him if he was on something. His emotions careened between terror and anger. Half the time he was mad as fuck that Dawson had bailed on him, that he'd run off instead of dealing with their issues. The rest of the time, Grady felt heartsick, fearing the worst, repeating a constant mantra of just one word—"please."

After a week, Grady was still despondent. Denny talked about hope and faith, but it felt too much like a deathwatch. He stopped in to visit Denny most evenings. From the haggard look on Denny's face, the shadowed eyes, the rapidly declining level in the gallon of whiskey on the kitchen counter, Grady knew Denny feared the worst.

By the second week, numbness settled in. Not knowing seemed worse than confirmation, but Grady dreaded the call that would end all doubt. He lurched between fantasizing about Dawson's safe return and their reunion, to preparing himself to grieve his death. The whipsaw of emotions left him exhausted. He couldn't concentrate worth shit in class. The auto shop gave him the week off.

The photos that had been a consolation now seemed flat and lifeless, and he couldn't bear to look at them. He'd never really thought about the possibility of Dawson not coming home, not being with him. This separation had been temporary, a way for them both to get their heads screwed on right. It was never meant to be forever. Grady's memories of Dawson were full of vibrant life, rich color, and raucous sound. But when he tried to imagine the future, all he saw was a blank slate.

When someone came to the door of his classroom to pull him out, Grady feared the worst. He wasn't sure his legs would support him, but he made it to the hallway, palms sweaty, heart thudding.

"Your uncle called and said to check your phone. It's important," the front office administrative assistant told him.

Grady's hand shook as he pulled the phone from his pocket and saw a message. Not daring to listen to the voicemail, he called back.

"Grady. He's alive. They just called me. I don't know more. But he's alive, and that's good enough."

Grady leaned against the wall and sank to the floor, tears running down his face. The admin watched him worriedly. "Bad news?"

He shook his head, drunk on relief. "No. It's good. It's all good."

When the email finally came a few days later, Dawson hadn't been able to tell them much. But to Grady, just knowing Dawson was alive and well enough to send the message healed a hole in his heart.

If he'd had any question about whether his love for Dawson was real, the past two weeks had burned them away. And from the tone of the response, Grady sensed that the near-death experience had made up Dawson's mind as well.

Just one more year, and they could finally work this out —together.

———

Present Day

Grady pulled himself out of his thoughts, combed his wet hair, and threw his dirty clothing in the hamper. The smell of lasagna filled the air, appealing even though Grady wasn't sure he could eat much. Still, he knew he needed to make an effort. He faked a smile and headed downstairs.

When he reached the kitchen, he saw Dawson and Denny sitting at the table.

"You didn't have to wait for me," he said, sorry he had needed so much time to pull himself together.

"Dawson was just catching me up on the news, so we didn't have to rehash it over dinner." Denny gestured toward the counter, where a do-it-yourself buffet awaited with salad, garlic bread, and the steaming deep dish pan of lasagna. "Go make plates. There are plenty of cookies for dessert."

Grady shot Dawson a grateful glance, relieved that he didn't have to recount the story or hear his partner's take on what had happened. Dawson smiled back and bumped his arm with an elbow in silent solidarity. Denny's clenched jaw told Grady that his uncle hadn't liked what he had heard, or worse yet, might share Dawson's worry.

How do I prove to them that I'm not a total mess? If I just sit around here waiting to "heal" I'll go stir-crazy. Work will help. Maybe that's it. Get my mind off things, stay busy.

"Gotta say, I'm looking forward to going back to the shop," Grady said after he had shoveled down a few forkfuls of food. He didn't have an appetite, but he knew the others were watching him, gauging his health by how much he ate, and Grady resolved to pass the test, even if he had to fight later to keep everything down.

"They worked out a schedule for us so we can ride together." Dawson made it sound like no big deal. "Sundays off, done by six most nights, half-day on Wednesday. With some wiggle room if an urgent hunt comes up."

Denny glared at Dawson at that last comment, and Dawson gave his best ingratiating smile. Grady got the definite feeling that Dawson and Denny had not seen eye-to-eye about things while he was in the shower.

"I want to see you work your magic at that fancy computer rig they bought you," Dawson said. "You'll need to show me how it works and impress me with your educated geekiness."

"There's not that much to see," Grady answered, secretly pleased at Dawson's interest. "Nothing as dramatic as putting a car up on a lift or pulling out an engine."

"Doesn't have to be dramatic," Dawson replied. "It's a valuable addition to the shop. I hope you made them pay you big bucks."

"Since you're both part-owners, you can always take it up with management when you shave in the morning," Denny put in, rolling his eyes.

The conversation over the rest of the meal stayed light, news about what was happening in the area, an update on how the peppers and tomatoes were coming along in Denny's garden, and what family gossip had come Denny's way through the grapevine.

Angel finished his kibble, tried to beg for a handout, and then settled in under the table, hoping for food to fall. When that failed to produce a snack, he trudged away to claim his spot on the couch.

After they cleaned up dinner, they headed into the living room. Denny poured three glasses of Jack, and Dawson snagged the plate of cookies and brought it as well, careful to put it well out of Angel's reach.

Denny settled into his favorite chair, which left Dawson and

Grady to share the couch with Angel. After a good-natured debate over which title to pick, Denny started the movie, and they settled in to cheer and jeer the hapless heroes of *Tremors*.

"Does it ever strike you as odd when we relax watching a monster movie?" Grady asked, sipping his whiskey and letting the burn soothe him.

"It's not exactly like we're watching a training film," Dawson pointed out, and Denny snorted in agreement. "It's pretty clear most of the time that the writers and the effects people haven't looked at any real lore. If we drank a shot every time they got the monsters or the weapons wrong, we'd have alcohol poisoning before the credits rolled."

"Having a sick sense of humor in this business isn't a requirement, but it helps," Denny added.

Angel shifted, laying his huge head in Grady's lap, eyes upturned to beg for an ear scratch. Grady relented, and the dog sighed with contentment.

"Looks like you two bonded," Dawson said. Grady swore heard the unspoken *while I was gone.*

"Angel's a bit of an opportunist if you hadn't noticed," Grady replied fondly. Not that the Rottweiler couldn't be a fearsome protector when the need arose. He'd seen Angel turn into a total badass against both human and supernatural threats. "He's just in touch with his softer side, aren't you, boy?" Angel's entire backside waggled in agreement.

"I think he's buttering you up to get your cookies," Dawson teased.

"They have chocolate. He can't have them."

"He's more of an eat-first, regret it later kind of dog," Denny pointed out.

Grady found his shoulders finally relaxing. This felt so normal, so *right* that he almost pinched himself to make sure it wasn't a dream.

The whiskey calmed his raw nerves, and while he'd started eating the lasagna out of stubbornness, he'd enjoyed the meal, and it sat with a comfortable heaviness in his stomach. He could also sense Dawson's presence sitting just a foot away, and longed to be able to slide closer, connected from knee to hip, and lean his head on Dawson's shoulder.

Someday. After I prove I'm not coming apart at the seams.

By the time the movie ended, Grady felt warm and boneless. Angel lay upside-down, legs in the air, snoring and drooling. Denny clicked off the TV, and they all carried dishes out to the kitchen.

"There's a coffee cake in the blue container on the counter if you want to grab something for breakfast on your way out. I set the coffee maker, so it should run a pot in the morning, assuming the timer works," Denny told them. "Don't expect that kind of service every day. Just figured your first day back on the job deserved it," he added with a smirk.

They thanked him and headed up to bed while he puttered downstairs for a while. Grady glanced at the clock and realized that it wasn't nearly as late as it felt, but then again, the day had gone hard on him.

"See you in the morning," Dawson told him when they parted ways in the hallway. "Don't forget to set an alarm." He looked like he wanted to say something more, maybe ask how Grady was holding up, but he didn't, which made Grady relieved and disappointed in equal measure.

"Don't let the bedbugs bite," Grady replied with a grin, repeating the line Denny had always told them when they were kids and had stayed over while their fathers went on a hunt.

Maybe before too long, they could end the evening with a kiss goodnight, Grady thought. Even better would be not needing to go their separate ways. *Guess one of us will need to get a place if it comes to that because Denny might not mind us getting together, but he's not going to want to hear it under his roof.*

He made short work of getting ready for bed and slipped under the covers. For once, instead of cycling through the hunts gone wrong, Grady's mind focused on a more pleasant problem.

Daw and I could afford a place if we pooled our money—assuming it didn't work out to stay in Dad's house. There are some decent cabins that come up for sale, even some of the places the seasonal people buy and then get tired of. That way we could be close, so Denny wouldn't be on his own too much, and we'd be handy to the shops and for hunting.

Grady drifted off to sleep, mentally furnishing a honeymoon cabin.

Dawson woke them all at two in the morning, screaming bloody murder as his nightmares caught up with him.

———

ANOTHER WEEK WENT BY, AND THEN TWO MORE. GRADY AND DAWSON fell into a new normal, getting up early to be settled at the auto shop before the opening rush, sharing their lunch break when the workload permitted, and jokingly griping about difficult customers on the way home.

Dawson and Denny made plans for them all to go to the Highland Games, a Scottish heritage festival with plenty of good food, locally-brewed mead, caber tossing, and bagpipes. One of Denny's friends loaned them a tent so they could stay on the festival grounds, and promised to take care of Angel while they were gone.

Grady had been skeptical at first, but the perfect weather and high spirits of the group made for a fun couple of days.

By the following weekend, Grady felt antsy for a hunt. He'd heard Denny on his phone, and he knew there had been incidents worth looking into and problems to handle. While most of the extended King family hunted, few did so full-time. Most of their relations had families and jobs, but with enough hunters in the area, they rarely had trouble finding someone to handle a problem.

After that last disastrous hunt, no one had mentioned them going out again. Dawson had been evasive about his nightmare, then admitted he had relived the hunt with a different ending, one where Grady didn't make it out. He had looked so worn and worried that Grady knew Dawson needed some space to process.

But the past weeks since they'd been back to work had gone

smoothly, no nightmares for either of them. Grady knew he wouldn't ever be truly "over" his father's death, and some days were harder than others, but he no longer felt crippled by the memory or the guilt. Whatever horrors haunted Dawson's dreams from his time in the military also seemed to fade, or at least were held at bay, although Grady figured that they, too, might never completely go away.

Then maybe we'll be two old crotchety men, bitching at each other about whose fault it is no one gets any sleep, he thought with a chuckle. He wanted that future so badly he could taste it.

The only thing worrying him was that despite the quiet weeks, Dawson hadn't made any moves to even tiptoe into the next phase. He laughed at Grady's jokes, seemed comfortable enough spending time together, and couldn't hide the evidence that he noticed Grady's blatant, light-hearted flirting. Grady hadn't pushed, but he also did his best to send "ready" signals at every opportunity.

Dawson didn't seem distant—he just didn't get closer. That vexed Grady, and he even debated talking to Uncle Denny, but he knew the last thing Denny wanted was to be put in the middle of their romantic problems. There wasn't anyone else Grady trusted enough to ask for advice, no one that he wanted up in his personal business. That left him to work it out for himself since Dawson had been conversational about everything except when they might take off the parking brake on the romantic side of their relationship and start rolling.

On bad days Grady worried that Dawson had changed his mind. Sometimes he could talk himself out of that; other days his heart wouldn't listen to reason. Whenever he was just about to bring it up and ask Dawson straight out, something always seemed to come up.

It didn't help that as Grady's mood leveled out, his libido woke up. Not that he hadn't been plenty horny since Dawson's return, but for a while nothing seemed the way it used to be. Food hadn't tasted as good, beer didn't help him relax, and jacking off relieved tension but didn't deliver any real satisfaction. He'd chalked it up to grief, anxiety, and depression, but now that he had started to feel more like his old self, Grady was increasingly impatient to explore this thing between them, the way he and Dawson originally planned.

The longer they went without either talking about it or shaking things up, the more an edge of anger crept in, beneath all the other emotions. Was Dawson coddling him? Did he still see Grady as too young, too fragile, or too immature to handle getting involved? Why was Grady doing all the work to get this off the ground, and why was Dawson making a decision that affected both of them, without at least talking to Grady?

So when he caught up with Dawson after they finished their shift at the garage that Friday, Grady had a plan in mind.

"I found a hunt," he announced when they headed home.

"Oh yeah?" Dawson sounded skeptical. Grady plunged ahead.

"Nothing too dangerous. More like taking care of a nuisance, really."

"That's what we said the last couple of times." Dawson's fingers tightened around the steering wheel.

"Hunts don't come rated like video games," Grady pointed out with an exaggerated sniff that got a hint of a smile in response, perhaps despite Dawson's better judgment.

"How'd you find it?"

"Heard some guys talking down at the shop while they were waiting on their cars. There's a bridge where a woman—Annie Gleason—supposedly drowned herself and her baby back during the Depression. Ever since, people have heard a baby crying at certain times when they cross."

Dawson shrugged. "There's a 'Crybaby Bridge' in just about every county. Probably an urban legend."

Grady had been prepared to be turned down. "The thing is, that road construction over on Big Bend Road needed a detour, so they've pushed traffic to the route with the Gleason Bridge—the one with the ghost. It's on a side road that usually only gets local use since the better highway went in. Now, more people are hearing the story, so there's been a lot of legend trippers, and the bridge is turning into a late-night hangout—which has attracted its own set of problems."

"Sounds more like Sheriff Rollins's kind of thing." Dawson shifted in his seat to rest his left arm on the Mustang's door.

"Rollins and his wolves have their hands full dealing with that den of coyote-shifter meth-heads," Grady countered. "And the reason the legend trippers keep going to the Gleason Bridge is that they're actually seeing, hearing, and getting video of the ghost."

That got Dawson's attention. "Seriously?"

Grady nodded. "Which brings even more traffic—you get the idea." He didn't mention that as the sightings continued, the ghost seemed to get more agitated, going from merely making an appearance to causing electronics to fail, frosting over windows, and shoving people who were carrying on too loudly.

Ghosts that could interact with the living posed a danger because no one could predict their actions, and the spirits' growing power often turned them vengeful. Grady suspected that while true paranormal investigators who went to the bridge were quiet and well-behaved, this new group of thrill-seekers turned the site of Annie Gleason's tragedy into a party, and she had started to punish them for their disrespectfulness.

If I tell Dawson she's actually dangerous, he'll decide we shouldn't go. Fuck that. Compared to the things we used to hunt when we were teenagers, this is a milk run. We need a win. Annie hasn't done anything really bad—yet. We can stop the ghost, make the nuisance go away, spare the cops some trouble, and get our mojo back.

"What do you think we're going to do about it? Go out there in broad daylight—or show up in the middle of the party crowd?"

Grady ground his teeth at Dawson's uncharacteristic lack of enthusiasm. Before these past couple of hunts, Dawson was always gung-ho to investigate, even if a rumor turned out to be nothing. Grady fought to tamp down the curl of anger that rose with every push back. *Does he lack confidence in himself—or in me?*

"Next time, I'm going to come armed with a PowerPoint and handouts," Grady joked, sounding a little brittle, even to himself. "I figured we go out at the ass crack of dawn, in between when the partiers have gone home and traffic picks up for the day. Probably take us fifteen minutes, tops."

Dawson gave him a wary look. "Why do you want to do this so badly? Aren't you enjoying having a little time off from getting thrown around and almost killed?"

"The longer we're out of the game, the harder it will be to get back in," Grady replied in a level voice. "We're Kings. We hunt monsters. Sometimes we get hurt. That goes with the job. I'm not ready to give up our legacy. Anyone can take a course and do what I do at the auto shop. But not everyone can hunt the things that go bump in the night. We trained for this. We were raised to it."

Grady's voice grew louder as the passion welled up inside him, bringing real heat to an argument he hadn't intended to make. "Ten generations of Kings on Cunanoon Mountain, Daw. All of them hunters. People look to our family to keep them safe. That's a responsibility I'm not ready to walk away from. It's part of who we are, Daw." *And wasn't that rich,* Grady thought, *coming from the son of the adopted guy who had always struggled to feel like a "real" King.*

Grady really did mean the words that poured out, even as he realized that playing the "responsibility" card on Dawson wasn't fair. Dawson was one of the most responsible souls Grady had ever met. He tried to take care of everyone around him, especially Grady.

Grady opened his mouth to apologize, to say that he was sorry for going too far when that curl of anger surfaced once more, and he clamped his lips together. *I might have laid it on a little thick, but it's still true. We can't just give up and walk away. And it's not like I'm suggesting we go after a nest of vampires or something. Baby steps. That's all. Ease our way back in.*

He could almost hear the internal argument in Dawson's mind, gleaned from the pinch of his eyes, the set of his mouth, and the play of emotions in his expression. And he knew the moment when Dawson gave in, from the way he slumped, just a bit, in defeat.

"Okay," Dawson said warily. "But that's a long-ass drive from here. So how about we drive over Saturday when we get off work and check the place out before the crazy people show up? Then we grab a bite to eat, stay over in a motel, and that way we can get a decent few hours' sleep before we go up against Annie, instead of wandering in groggy as hell and half awake."

"That works for me." Before Dawson went off to the Army, they used to stay in small motels fairly often when the hunt required it. Grady hadn't been going to suggest staying over. But it had occurred to him that maybe Dawson resisted moving their relationship forward, in part, because he didn't want to make Denny uncomfortable. Maybe having a room to themselves, an easy hunt, and a victory celebration of sorts would help Dawson get over his reservations and see that it was time to make this thing happen between them.

Dawson didn't talk as much as he usually did on the rest of the ride home, and when Grady tried to break the silence with comments or questions, his partner's answers were short, with no follow-up.

He didn't sound angry, Grady thought, trying to riddle out the other man's headspace. Apprehensive, maybe? That didn't make any sense. *Daw's been in a war zone. He was pretty badass before he left, and he should be even more solid about knowing how to go up against an enemy now, with more training and experience. I don't get it. Is he tired of hunting altogether? Is it still the ambush haunting him, or something else he never told us about?*

Grady thought about calling off the hunt since Dawson's heart didn't seem to be in it. He didn't want to be selfish or put Dawson in harm's way.

"Look, if you want to sit this one out, it's okay," Grady ventured when they pulled in at Denny's house. "I can probably get Colt to go with me."

Dawson turned to him with an unreadable expression. "When have you ever hunted with Colt?"

"Quite a few times, actually, while you were gone. When Dad had to be somewhere else." This time, his irritation at Dawson counteracted the stab of grief that came from mentioning his father. "We did okay."

Did he see a flare of jealousy in Dawson's eyes? Hard to believe, since Dawson hadn't been in a hurry to be anything but friends. That hadn't been Grady's goal, and he didn't want this to go off the rails.

"I mean, it was never as much fun as going with you, but we got the job done," Grady said, attempting a save. "I just thought that, if you really didn't want to go, it's an option."

With the Mustang parked and turned off, Denny would be wondering soon why they didn't come in. Dawson shifted in his seat, turning an assessing look on Grady that he usually saved for questioning witnesses.

"Why does this matter so much to you? What are you trying to prove? And who are you trying to prove it to—you or me?"

A sting of hurt accompanied the rush of annoyance. "It matters because we made all these plans to go on hunts and do all kinds of things, and we aren't doing them. I'm not messed up like I was. Neither of us is hurt. This is a chance to help. We never used to think twice about a job like this. I just feel like..." He struggled for the right words, realizing he was dangerously close to saying things he couldn't take back.

"I feel like we've gotten lost somewhere. With you and me...hunting," he hurried to add. "And I don't know if you've changed your mind, or if something's bothering you, or if I did something to make you mad, but, I just want everything to work out," Grady wrapped up, feeling like he'd just blown everything, as if he'd said far too much. He held his breath, waiting for Dawson to respond.

Maybe this would finally break through Dawson's silence, and get him to tell Grady what was bothering him, costing him sleep, dogging him with nightmares. Grady couldn't shake the feeling there was something Dawson wasn't telling him, some secret that he hadn't confessed. Whatever it was, they could fix it, Grady felt certain they could, if only Dawson would tell him what was wrong.

"It'll work out," Dawson said, with a note of certainty in his voice and a smile that didn't reach his eyes. "And we're not lost—we're right where we're supposed to be," he added, with a gesture toward the house.

A joke? Grady felt indignation rise. *I spill my guts to him, and he makes a joke?* "I guess we are," Grady replied, his tone frosty. "My mistake." He was out of the car and up the steps before Dawson could object.

Grady tried to put the disagreement in the car behind them, but it colored his mood that evening despite his best efforts. Several times, he thought Dawson was about to say something, only to have the other man suddenly veer off to another topic. Denny glowered at both of them, and Grady wondered if they were on the verge of getting sent to clean out the tool shed together, their uncle's favorite punishment for fighting with each other when they were younger.

Conversation over dinner felt strained, although everyone talked, and Grady made an extra effort not to do anything that might be interpreted as "sulking." He pushed himself to recount a funny story about a mix-up with cars owned by two people with the same name, which almost had one man's wife picking up the wrong fellow. Under normal circumstances, that would have led to a chain of similar stories, but tonight, once the laughter died, they all picked awkwardly at their plates.

Grady took the lead on clearing the table and feeding Angel. "Hey, they just added that action flick we missed when it was in the theater," he said, hoping that streaming a movie might ease the tension. "I heard it's good. Last one on the couch has to take Angel out for his bedtime walk!"

They settled into their usual seats, including Angel, and the show proved to be as good as its hype. Grady felt the tension fade a bit. Still, Dawson seemed to be preoccupied, not making as many smartass remarks as usual, or the risqué side comments he usually stage-whispered to Grady. Denny kept his focus on the screen as if he was fed up with their drama.

Grady split his attention between Angel and the TV, although neither fully distracted him. The more he thought about the conversation in the car, the more he felt sure he had lost by winning. Still, maybe if the hunt at the bridge went smoothly, if he could remind Dawson how good they were together, maybe it would break them out of whatever kind of limbo they'd been stuck in.

Dawson seemed to be just as tired as Grady felt when they parted in the upstairs hallway, although his gaze lingered a bit too long as if there was something he wanted to say. Grady waited, holding his breath.

Dawson's eyes shuttered, locking in whatever admission he might have made. "G'night," he said, looking down and away before heading into his room.

The door shut before Grady had the chance to reply.

———

THE NEXT MORNING BOTH GRADY AND DAWSON SEEMED TO BE MAKING an extra effort to keep the conversation light and the mood pleasant on the way to work. They didn't mention the hunt, although Grady had researched well into the night since he couldn't sleep. If Dawson had nightmares, they weren't bad enough to wake anyone else, and he lacked the tension around his eyes that Grady associated with his worst nights.

Even though they didn't talk about Annie Gleason and the haunted bridge, both men brought an overnight duffel so they could leave from work, and Dawson put their gear bag with the weapons in the trunk, just in case. Denny was in the kitchen when they left, and wished them luck, before reminding them not to be stupid.

Saturday was busy, and Grady was slammed with appointments all day. He had no idea why half the cars in the valley seemed to have picked that day to come in for service, but he figured it might have had something to do with it being nice weather and a good reason to be out. From what he saw of the main bays, Dawson's part of the shop had an equally crazy schedule. Neither of them took a lunch break, and Grady washed down his sandwich with a soda in between customers.

By closing time, Grady needed coffee almost as much as he needed a good meal. He picked up two large cups to-go right after work to tide them over on the drive. When he made their reservation at a small mom-and-pop motel near the Gleason bridge, Grady had also checked the restaurants nearby. He found a local diner with great ratings, as well as a vintage breakfast restaurant that specialized in pancakes and waffles for the next morning.

Dawson looked worn when he started the Mustang and headed out of town. Grady told him about the motel and the two restaurants he had found, hoping to stoke a bit of enthusiasm. Dawson thanked him for the coffee and for setting everything up, asked a few polite questions about the menus, and then seemed to get lost in the highway and the music.

That alone wasn't completely unusual. They'd logged a lot of miles together, and there wasn't always much to talk about. Grady often napped, reviewed notes, or played on his phone if they had decent cell service.

Tonight, something still felt off, although Grady swore they were both trying to be on their best behavior. That alone worried him because he'd never felt the need to behave a certain way with Dawson. The easiness between them always seemed to come naturally, and Grady didn't know where things had gone wrong.

He thought about asking Dawson what was on his mind and decided against it. Dawson had shot him down—jokingly—the previous night. He didn't seem any more forthcoming now, and Grady didn't want to put them on a worse footing than they already were. He hoped Dawson would spill when he was ready, but Grady's patience had begun to fray.

Things almost seemed back to normal over dinner. The diner, or at least part of it, was in a real old-fashioned trolly car like Grady had seen on TV. According to the short history on the menu, the place had been part of the local scenery for decades.

"Did you see what she just put down on that table?" Dawson asked, watching as the server unloaded her tray a few tables over. "That all looks amazing."

"I sorta want one of everything," Grady admitted.

"And those desserts—in the case up front?" Dawson hadn't taken his eyes off the five-layer chocolate cake with chocolate icing, as if it might vanish before he could order.

Grady ordered a double bacon cheeseburger with homemade onion rings, and Dawson got the blue-plate special meatloaf and mashed potatoes. They went ahead and ordered dessert at the same time, to make sure to get their first choices. Grady's banana cream pie was the best he'd ever eaten, while Dawson said the same about the five-layer chocolate cake.

The conversation came a little easier over dinner, and Grady thought maybe they had both been tired and hungry. He knew, deep down, that didn't account for everything, but he was trying, dammit.

Even the coffee tasted better than usual, and Grady couldn't believe he'd lived in these hills all his life without ever having heard of the place, but they both promised to come back the next time they were in the area.

They drove past the bridge, wanting to get the lay of the land before they came out to dispel Annie's ghost the next morning. The two-lane road had more traffic than it was designed to carry, thanks to the detour. It didn't help that half a dozen cars congregated on the berm on either side of an old concrete bridge.

"I can see why it's a nuisance," Dawson said, slowing the Mustang enough for them to take in the scene.

The thrill-seekers had set up a tailgate party, barely off the road far enough to avoid getting hit. Drivers slowed to get a look at what was going on, which presented a danger in itself. The loud laughter and bright headlights certainly weren't intended for optimal ghost-watching.

At the hotel, it didn't take long to get everything ready for the morning. Grady made sure they had extra salt and holy water, in case Annie's ghost resisted being sent on her way.

Maybe she's not vengeful. Maybe she just wants a good night's sleep, Grady thought, remembering the obnoxious legend trippers.

"Were the bodies of Annie and her child ever recovered?" Dawson asked, after getting Grady to go over the details again. Grady took that interest as a good sign.

"No."

"Then how do we banish the ghosts? It's not like an exorcism."

"The guy at the shop who was talking about Annie said she was a relative. He knew I was a King, so when I asked him some questions, he said he'd always felt bad that Annie and her baby had been stuck there for so long. Told me his mother had a needlepoint sampler that Annie supposedly stitched and a christening gown she had embroidered for the baby. When I said I'd be willing to try to get them to cross over, he offered to give those to us, to make it work."

Grady produced the two items from a large envelope in the bag. The simple white dress had yellowed with age, but Annie's fine needlework was still visible in the design along the hem. The sampler was a piece of muslin with fine, close stitching to create a scene with flowers and bees, showcasing Annie's skill.

"They aren't bones, but they were personal possessions, and both would have had a deep emotional connection, if not exactly to the baby, then to Annie."

"Nice work." Dawson looked impressed. "I don't imagine the ice cream stand a bit farther up the road is going to be happy when we get rid of their star attraction. Want to bet at least some of the people who come ghost hunting stop for a shake on the way home?"

"They can dress someone up like a ghost and have them pop out from under the bridge," Grady replied. "At least Annie and Catherine will be able to rest."

Something in the gear bag caught Dawson's attention, and he reached inside, pulling out a bundle of sage and white roses.

"Not exactly our go-to banishing kit," he said, with a glance toward Grady. When he reached in again, he had a stoppered bottle of sanctified oil, like they had used against the baleful ghost of the phantom train. "Did you just decide to be extra-careful, or were there some details you might have left out of the story?"

"After what happened before, I figured it was good not to take any chances," Grady replied, feeling a mixture of chagrin at being caught and annoyance that he'd felt the need to hold back in the first place.

Grady sighed. "Since the tailgaters have been partying at the bridge, there've been reports about Annie doing more than just showing up and then vanishing. Maybe she thinks they're being disrespectful."

"What kind of stories?"

"They might not be true. Since the bridge got popular, people might be coming up with tall tales to get attention."

"Try me."

"Windows frosting over, making cell phones not work, shoving a guy. Not exactly slasher flick stuff."

"You knew she could be dangerous? Why didn't you say so?"

Grady turned away. "Because I was afraid you wouldn't come. I thought maybe if we just got our routine going again, it would go easier, okay? And we've handled much worse things than wonky electronics or iced-over windows."

"It looks like you brought the right stuff," Dawson said. "Can't think of anything you missed. Hope we don't need it." He didn't sound angry, just a little melancholy. Or maybe disappointed.

"Thanks." Grady put the christening gown and sampler back in the envelope and returned them to the bag. "Look, I'm sorry. I should have told you everything. And I meant what I said—if you don't want to do this, we can go home. Deal with it another time."

"With Colt?"

Grady threw his hands in the air. "With someone who wants to do the hunt. Hell, maybe Denny would come with me, or one of the relations. Or we can leave Annie be, and forget I ever brought it up. Maybe I can do this myself."

Dawson was watching Grady with that intense focus that always made him feel exposed, and not in a sexy way. "You'd do this without me?"

"I don't want to. I want to hunt *with* you. But that means you have to want to hunt," Grady hated the tone in his voice, halfway between frustration and pleading.

"If Annie's gaining power and interacting, she's a danger. We have to get her to let go," Dawson said. "And I want to hunt with you too. Always have."

"Hasn't seemed like it, lately," Grady muttered, angry at himself for not hiding the hurt.

"There's been a lot going on," Dawson replied. He reached back to rub his neck; a sure tell that he wasn't showing all his cards. "I told you—it will all work out." That conviction didn't seem to reach his eyes.

"So, are we still on?" Grady asked, mustering his game face. He couldn't help feeling frustrated, and he'd probably fucked things up between them even worse than before, but at least Dawson knew the whole story. He didn't like keeping secrets.

Except for the invisible elephant in the room, the fact that I'm long overdue for wanting to kiss some sense into him and then have hot, sweaty make-up sex. And it would be nice if it happened sometime before I'm old enough for those little blue pills.

"Yes, we're on. Came all this way, got a nice room and everything," Dawson replied with a hint of a smile. "Even bought you dinner."

"Never let it be said that I'm a cheap date." The words were out of Grady's mouth before he could stop them. He felt himself blush. Dawson flinched, just barely, but Grady saw.

"Hey, I'll even buy breakfast too. Because I'm that kind of guy," Dawson quipped. His heart didn't seem in it, although they both laughed.

"I wasn't kidding about getting up at the ass-crack of dawn," Grady warned. "Which is going to seem way too soon. I'm going to get cleaned up, and then crash." The room had a double bed and a pull-out couch. "I'll take the couch."

Maybe someday I won't have to. But the way things are going, it won't be nearly as soon as I'd like.

————

AT FOUR-THIRTY IN THE MORNING, THE SUN HADN'T RISEN, BUT THE tailgaters had finally gone to bed, leaving a mess of empty beer cans, take-out containers, and a few other things Grady didn't want to examine too closely. They played the beams of their flashlights over the area, looking for stragglers or wild animals, but nothing stirred.

A mist rose from the creek that ran under the bridge. The stream didn't look like much now, but after the spring rains, it could be swift and treacherous, as it had been the night Annie jumped with her baby.

Dawson and Grady approached cautiously, expecting Annie to attack. They could hear the running stream, the wind overhead, the crunch of their boots on the old road. Nothing seemed amiss.

Maybe Annie wore herself out pranking the tailgaters, Grady thought. *Hope that makes our jobs a little easier.*

Grady set out the items for the ritual while Dawson kept watch. They were armed, not knowing what to expect. Dawson had the shotgun, both men carried knives of iron and silver, and they scattered salt in a wide area to give themselves a safe base and to keep Annie from sneaking up on them.

This time Grady wasn't taking any chances. They usually didn't do a full ritual to dispel ghosts, simply because most spirits were just a little confused and needed a nudge, or maybe permission to go on. But the troublesome spirits, those bent on revenge or bound by remorse or the ones who just couldn't accept that they were dead— needed something stronger.

Grady knew the ritual by heart, and he'd practiced the set up a few times before they left home, just to be sure. He laid down a circle of salt large enough for him and Dawson and placed rune-carved candles at the quarters. Grady chalked sigils on the road beside each candle, and then added a pinch of boxwood, sage, and cloves to each as he lit them.

He knelt in the center of the circle with a blessed silver bowl. Beside it, he laid the bundle of sage and white roses, as well as the rest of the items they needed. Dawson held onto the vial of blessed oil, as a back-up.

The ritual drew from a variety of traditions. Smoke from the candles carried the scent of the protective herbs aloft, filling the air.

Grady drew a couple of grounding breaths, focusing on the candle flames to center himself.

"Here we go," he murmured.

"Do it. I've got your back."

Grady lifted a silver flask of holy water above the bowl, pouring a thin stream as he spoke. "I call the ghost of Annie Gleason, and her child, Catherine. It is long past the time for your spirits to move on. We bid you to release your hold on the mortal world and take your eternal rest."

Next, he took the stopper from a small stoneware jug of sanctified communion wine. "I beseech you, in the name and by the power of all you hold holy, to renounce the ills that bind you here and enter the next realm." The wine swirled with the water, as Grady lifted the last ingredient, a palmful of graveyard dirt from the Gleason family plot.

"Those who wronged you are long dead. Those who renounced the child paid for their arrogance. You are avenged, and your family claims you and the child as their own. There is no power binding you to this place except your guilt. Let go and be free."

He had a few more incantations up his sleeve, in case Annie didn't want to listen, or had faded too far for reason.

"Looks like your call went through."

Dawson's murmur made Grady look up to see a young, dark-haired woman in a plain white shift holding a baby against her chest. She might have been his own age or younger, he thought, taking in her drenched clothing, sodden hair, and the wild, grief-stricken look in her eyes. The child in her arms didn't move. Grady wondered if the legend had gotten the details wrong. Maybe Anne didn't kill her child. Maybe she *joined* a child she already lost.

A shriek split the night, full of madness and fury. Annie's ghost rushed at Grady, one hand out and ready to claw him with her nails. Grady took a deep breath to remain calm and began the Latin rite of banishment.

"Just tell me when you want me to shoot," Dawson growled, ready with the shotgun and oil to dispel the spirit. Grady shook his head in warning. They had Annie's attention, and so long as the salt line remained unbroken, she couldn't hurt them.

Their flashlights flickered, then the glow faded, although both had fresh batteries. The candles gave enough light to see by, although Grady had brought an old-fashioned torch with a gas-soaked rag, just in case.

Both men jumped when the horn in the Mustang blared, and the headlights turned on and off as the wipers swept back and forth.

Grady's chant never faltered, finishing the Latin rite and following up with an old Celtic litany to free the restless dead.

The wind picked up, swirling dead leaves and road dust around the protected circle. Annie edged closer; eyes fixed on Grady.

"Grady, the salt!"

Dawson's warning came a second too late, as the warded barrier thinned and then broke. Annie surged closer, closing her bony hand around Grady's wrist. He gasped, feeling her drawing off his energy, but did not stop the chant.

The boom of the shotgun almost deafened Grady, and the smell of gunpowder filled the air. Annie's ghost vanished, and Grady stepped back. Dawson filled in the small gap in the circle and racked another shot in the shotgun.

"Better hurry," Dawson urged. Grady nodded, proud that despite the attack, he hadn't broken the litany.

Grady lit the torch and burned the bundle of sage and the dried white rose, sprinkling the ashes into the mixture in the bowl. Next, he pulled out the embroidered sampler and the christening gown.

"Annie and Catherine, by the powers of earth and sky, fire and water, and all you once held sacred, be at rest!"

He held the items above the flames, watching them catch. As the fire consumed them, Annie's ghost took form once more, a little farther away. Grady made sure that the ashes fell into the bowl and sank into the consecrated liquid.

"Look!"

At Dawson's prompt, Grady lifted his head to see Annie standing much closer. But the ghost's appearance had changed. She wore a flowered dress, hair neatly combed and pulled back, and the child in her arms was bundled in a pink knitted blanket. But what struck Grady was the expression of peace that eased Annie's features. Her eyes were sad and wistful, but the madness was gone.

Annie raised a hand in farewell, and then she and Catherine vanished.

Grady slumped forward, drained.

"Gray? Talk to me. Did she hurt you?" Dawson hadn't relaxed his vigil, keeping the gun leveled in case another threat appeared. That was good, Grady thought because he wasn't much up to kicking ass right now.

"I'm good," he said. "And she didn't have a grip on me for long. Stole some energy, that's all." He looked down at his wrist, which clearly held the whitish outline of a small hand as if he'd gotten mild frostbite.

"Let's get out of here."

"Gotta release the wardings, and then I'm all for that." Grady poured the mixture from the chalice into a clean mason jar with sigils scratched on its sides and screwed the cap on tightly. Denny would know how to deal with it later. Then he spoke the words of an incantation to dispel the protections as he blew out the candles and scattered the salt and herbs. When the energy had dissipated, Grady gathered up the items and packed them carefully in his bag.

Dawson put a hand on his shoulder. "Are you okay?"

Grady nodded, feeling scraped raw inside from the emotional ritual. The momentary contact with Annie had given him a flash of her memories and a jolt of her emotional turmoil. He didn't have words yet to describe it, and he knew Dawson would worry, so he just nodded. "Yeah, just tired."

"You did good back there," Dawson said as they got in the Mustang. The horn and lights had stopped when Annie disappeared, and thankfully her electrical hijinks hadn't drained the battery.

They rode for a while in silence, although Grady could tell Dawson had questions he could barely keep himself from asking.

"She didn't kill her baby."

Dawson's head turned sharply to look at him, before returning to watch the road. "What?"

"The baby was born dead. Annie wasn't married, and the child's father wouldn't claim her or the child. Her family turned their back. When Catherine was born dead, Annie had nowhere to go and nothing to live for. She hoped that she and Catherine could be together in heaven."

"And she got stuck under a bridge for almost a century instead? That really sucks." Dawson frowned. "How did you know all that?"

"When Annie grabbed me, she made a connection. All her memories—suddenly, I knew them. I could feel her fear and loss and desperation. Everyone turned their back on her, Daw. She was younger than we are."

Grady hadn't heard of another hunter being overtaken with a ghost's memories. He'd need to research that. The unexpected onslaught hadn't just shown him images; he had felt Annie's emotions like his own. The experience left him shaken, trying to sort out his own feelings from the rage, betrayal, disappointment, and bereavement projected into his thoughts.

Dawson watched him, and Grady knew the other man was trying to triage the injuries. "I'm not hurt," Grady protested. "Just some frostbite where she touched me." He figured the emotional piece would sort itself out with time.

A pink sunrise spread across the sky, and Grady's stomach rumbled. Dawson pulled into their motel and grabbed the first aid kit from the trunk.

"Show me your arm," Dawson said once they were inside their room. Grady obligingly pulled up his sleeve to reveal the already-fading marks.

"It's nothing. If it makes you feel better, I'll put some cream on them when I get out of the shower. I need to rinse everything off."

There was a reason rituals often began and ended with the officiant bathing or being purified. Psychic residue could cling to the person dispelling a dark power or troubled spirit, like blood splatter from a gunshot. Fortunately, soap and water were sufficient in most cases, and Grady couldn't wait to feel the hot water washing away the night's work.

"Alright," Dawson replied. "That pancake and waffle place you wanted to go to is just across the road. Since the sun's up, it's probably going to get busy. How about if I go get us a table and order coffee, and you come over as soon as you shower?"

Grady nodded, glad to have a little time to himself to sort through the ritual's aftermath. "Sounds good to me. Be sure you get cream for the coffee."

Dawson gave a thumbs-up and headed out the door.

Grady leaned against the cold tile, waiting for the water to get as hot as he could stand it. The small bar of soap nearly slipped through his hands time and again, but it smelled of rosemary and mint, both good for purification. He breathed deeply and murmured a short litany to release negative energy. Perhaps it was wishful thinking, but he felt a little better.

Still, he had a heavy heart as he toweled down and got dressed, not bothering to shave. Grady knew the ghost's touch had colored his mood, but he couldn't shake it off. Dawson had been protective and supportive, even though he hadn't originally wanted to do the hunt. He had seemed genuinely proud of Grady's ability to work the ritual, and concerned for his safety. But Dawson was hiding something, and Grady had begun to run out of ideas for how to bridge the gap between them. He seesawed between anger over seeming to be the only one of them making an effort and despair that he could ever set things right.

Grady packed his duffel bag so they could get on the road right after breakfast, although they had the room until noon. He left it on his bed, then laced his boots and shouldered into his jacket.

Even at this hour, a constant stream of tractor-trailers whizzed down the state highway between the motel and the pancake palace. Grady timed his run and dodged across, as the big rigs rumbled behind him, whipping up a wind in passing.

The breakfast spot already looked crowded, and the parking lot had few empty spaces. Through the big picture windows, Grady could see inside, and he started scanning for Dawson, hoping he had been able to get a table and wasn't still waiting up front.

He spotted Dawson and was about to head for the door when he realized Dawson wasn't alone. Grady froze, unable to look away. A good-looking blond man sat across from Dawson, and from their body language, Grady knew he wasn't a stranger to his partner, although Grady had never seen him before. The blond grinned as he said something, and Dawson smiled back. Then the man reached over and laid his hand on Dawson's, and Grady didn't have to read lips to guess the intent of the blond's next comment.

In that instant, Dawson looked toward the window and met Grady's gaze.

Grady bolted. He dodged the tour bus pulling into the parking lot and raced across the highway in a gap between the semis roaring past. Then he unlocked the door to the room, looking about wildly for pen and paper to scribble a note.

He didn't know who the man was in the diner, but he'd obviously been *someone* to Dawson. The glaring evidence that a stranger had shared a level of intimacy with Dawson that was still out of reach for Grady, on top of the raw emotions from the ritual and the clusterfuck of the past month, kicked Grady into flight mode.

Grady grabbed his duffel and locked the door behind him. He spotted a delivery truck just getting ready to pull out, and sprinted to catch up, begging to hitch a ride.

"Where d'ya need me to drop you, kid?" the driver asked.

Grady needed a minute to think. He couldn't go back to Denny's house, not until he'd sorted out his spiraling mood and breaking heart. Going back to his dad's house wasn't any better—Dawson would track him down, and Grady wasn't ready for that. The driver raised an eyebrow, and Grady blurted out the first thing that came to mind.

"I'm heading to Lake Toxaway," he said, remembering a friend's family cabin from years ago. "If you're heading in the general direction, I'd appreciate the lift."

"Got a couple of deliveries out that way, so you're in luck." The driver adjusted his cap and turned up the radio. "Hope you like Country music. That's the only station I play."

Grady figured it was just his luck and settled in for a drive filled with cheating lovers, broken promises, and shattered dreams, a playlist that seemed to be ripped from the headlines of his life.

9

DAWSON

Waffle Wonderland looked like it might be as good as the name promised. Dawson's stomach growled at the smell of bacon and maple syrup. Despite being just after dawn, the restaurant had filled fast. Coming early to hold a place had been a good idea.

The hostess led him to a table, and he asked for a pot of coffee, plenty of cream, and two mugs, making sure she knew he had someone joining him. Dawson breathed deeply, letting the sights and sounds wash over him, grateful he was no longer in the Army.

He and Grady had a ton of things to work out. Dawson knew Grady still operated on a ragged edge, one of the reasons he hadn't pressed to make good on his promises, much to the annoyance of his own very frustrated cock. Then again, Grady had done just fine banishing Annie Gleason's ghost, and Dawson had been impressed. Maybe they were closer to figuring things out than he had thought.

But why did he keep dreaming about the Black Shuck? He'd had another vision of the omen the night before they headed out, which made him doubly wary of the hunt. Annie's ghost had tried to hurt Grady, but they'd pushed her back fairly easily. He'd never been in serious danger. That just didn't make sense when the Shuck was such a potent harbinger of death.

Dawson wished he could tell Grady about the omens or at least ask Denny for advice. But he didn't want to risk it, not when he'd been told, at some point, that to speak of an omen was to bring it about. He knew that Grady suspected he was keeping a secret, which didn't help to repair the trust between them. He could see the suspicion in his partner's eyes and knew that worked against him.

I don't even know what threat the Shuck is warning me about. How can I keep Gray safe and not drive more of a wedge between us because I'm not telling him everything? He knew he would need to come up with an answer soon, or the whole situation could blow up in his face.

Dawson heard footsteps coming his way. Grady had to have set a land speed record to finish a shower this fast. He looked up, expecting to see his partner, only to have a different blond-haired, blue-eyed man slide into the seat across from him.

"Dawson! Haven't seen you in a long time."

"Hello, Corbin. Didn't expect to see you around here." Dawson tried to keep his manner easy, but inside, he saw trouble with a capital "T."

He remembered the man's first name, but not his last. Corbin had been one of Dawson's semi-regular fuck buddies in Asheville, before the Army. His resemblance to Grady, negative test results and his distinct lack of interest in commitment were the things that mattered most at the time. Corbin hadn't been bad company for an hour or two.

"What brings you out this way?" Corbin leaned back in the chair like he meant to settle in. He either hadn't noticed that the table was set for two, or didn't care.

"Business travel. You?"

Corbin shrugged. "Finished up a custom bike for a client and towed it out here for him. Came out pretty nice, if I do say so myself." He flashed a smile, and Dawson remembered that while Corbin was slicker and far more experienced than Grady, his dimples made the physical resemblance even stronger.

That had been a selling point before Dawson nearly had the real thing for his very own.

Dawson dredged up a memory that Corbin did custom motorcycle builds and paint jobs. A shared interest in everything mechanical had given them enough to talk about when they weren't otherwise occupied.

Grady's going to be here any minute. Shit, this is bad. I've got to get rid of Corbin without causing a scene. Never expected to see him again. Certainly not here.

"If you've got some free time, we could pick up where we left off." Corbin had never been the subtle type. He moved his hand to cover Dawson's.

"I'm meeting my boyfriend for breakfast," Dawson said, starting to pull his hand back. "I'm not on the market anymore."

Something made Dawson glance toward the window. He glimpsed Grady's face, knew from his expression that he'd seen Corbin make his move. Grady turned and ran. Dawson jerked his hand free like he'd been burned, but the damage was done.

"Gotta go," Dawson said, getting up and dropping a ten on the table to cover the pot of coffee and a generous tip.

Corbin grabbed his arm. It took all of Dawson's self-control not to shake him loose. "Can I call you?"

"I'm in a relationship." Dawson certainly hoped that would be true. Although this wasn't helping his odds with Grady. "So, no."

"Dawson—"

Dawson stepped back, forcing Corbin to loosen his hold or fall off his chair. "Sorry. Off the market. Have a safe drive home."

In the minutes since Grady ran off, a tour bus disgorged its passengers, and at least fifty seniors crowded the restaurant entranceway. Dawson tried to work his way toward the door through the tightly-clustered group, but the newcomers didn't want to lose their place in line, and those who were willing to shift didn't move quickly.

Even more people milled around the outside of the entrance, glaring as he tried to make his way past them.

"Excuse me," he murmured over and over again when he wanted to tell them all to get the fuck out of his way.

"So rude," one woman sniffed, reluctantly shifting although she was blocking the only path between the door and the sidewalk by standing next to the entranceway pillar.

Dawson muttered an apology, then sprinted toward the road as soon as he was free of the crowd. He waited while a seemingly never-ending line of tractor-trailers zoomed past.

"Fucking lousy time for a convoy," he growled. The trucks were going too fast and driving too close together for him to even think about making a run for it. When one side cleared, the other had a steady stream, and without a median island, Dawson had to wait for the magic moment traffic died down in both directions.

In hindsight, they should have just driven over together. He wouldn't make that mistake again, assuming there was a "next time."

Dawson reached the door to their room, alarmed when he found it locked. It had been less than ten minutes since his escape from the diner, and he had expected to find Grady angrily pacing.

The room was dark and empty. "Gray?"

His heart pounded when no answer came. Then he realized that Grady's bag was gone. He saw the hotel notepad lying next to his own duffel on the bed.

"I can't do this anymore."

Dawson stood, frozen, with the notepad in his hand. His heart thudded, and his mouth had gone dry. The coffee in his stomach threatened to make a return.

Fuck! I knew Grady was impatient, wanting to get things started. We needed to talk. But I couldn't tell him about the Black Shuck, not and keep him safe. I was afraid he'd come in and see Corbin, and we'd fight. I never thought he'd run off.

Now what do I do?

Dawson sank down onto the end of the bed and tried to pull himself together. He hadn't seen Grady anywhere on his way in, and the highway wasn't designed for pedestrians, so Dawson doubted Grady had just taken off on foot. He hadn't boosted the Mustang, and although they both knew how to hotwire a car from their work at the shop, that wasn't Grady's style.

It hurt like hell that Grady left without getting his side of the story, and part of him wanted to be angry that Grady didn't trust him more.

Then again, he trusted me about wanting us to take it slowly, but stick to our agreement. And it's been almost ten weeks without me making a move. But damn, it's been a fucking hard ten weeks with everything that happened, and I didn't want to screw things up when neither of us were a hundred percent.

Guess I managed to do that anyhow. How did he disappear so fast?

One look out the window gave Dawson a good idea as he watched the traffic go by, and saw a laundry truck pull out. All Grady had to do was hitch a ride with someone who was leaving, and he could be anywhere.

I've got to find him. He's in danger, and he doesn't realize it. This is all my fault—I need to make this right. After everything, I can't lose him. Not when we're so close to having what we both wanted.

Dawson tried to call Grady. It went straight to voice mail. He texted, figuring that was harder to ignore. *Grady—I didn't cheat. I turned him down, told him I was in a relationship. Please let me explain.* He saw that the text was delivered but not read.

Dawson sat with his head in his hands for a few minutes, thinking about what to do next. He picked up his phone again. Denny answered on the second ring.

"You boys okay?" Denny's gruff voice didn't hide his worry.

"I fucked up." Dawson stood and started to pace. Each time he passed the window and saw the trucks roaring by, he wondered how far Grady intended to run, and whether he was ever coming back.

"Nothing new about that. What's wrong?"

"Grady left."

The silence on the other end of the line made Dawson wonder if his uncle had lost the connection. "What do you mean, he 'left'?"

"He ditched me. His bag, everything is gone."

"That doesn't sound like Grady."

"He wrote a note." Reluctantly, Dawson read the short message aloud.

"Lovers' spat?"

"No! I mean, not really, because we aren't...we haven't—"

Denny's long-suffering sigh spoke volumes. "I was really hoping I wouldn't end up in the middle between you two. I'm not cut out to be Dr. Phil. But...I guess there's no helping it. How about you take it from the top, and fill me in."

Dawson told him about how things were on the drive out, and how well banishing Annie's ghost had gone. Explaining about Corbin at breakfast had his cheeks heating.

"Figures Grady would pick that moment to show up," Denny replied. "But if everything had been going well between the two of you up to that point, it's odd he'd just cut and run. Grady's too stubborn for that."

Dawson dropped into one of the molded plastic chairs by the table, which squeaked under his weight. "It's not just that. I mean, I think the thing with Corbin was the straw that broke the camel's back, but it's not the *only* thing."

"I couldn't help noticing you two dancing around each other these past weeks. And before you got home—well, at least before the werewolf and Aaron's death—Grady was so excited to see you again he couldn't contain himself. Kinda cute, although I'd never tell him that."

"We promised each other we would start dating when I got back, and see what came of it." Dawson didn't figure that was a surprise, but he felt his ears burn, just the same.

"Dating?" Denny echoed. "Maybe I gave you both credit for brains you don't have. My God, boy, the two of you have been making cow eyes at each other for years when you thought no one was looking. And you were waiting for the right moment to ask him on a *date*?"

"This isn't a hook-up or some kind of fling," Dawson defended himself. "I love him, Denny. I think I always have. If we do this, I want it to last forever."

"So where's the problem?"

"I had all kinds of plans for a big reunion when I got home. And then, when I found out about Aaron's death, and I saw how hard Grady was taking it, I knew it wasn't the right time to start things. He was vulnerable. I didn't want to take advantage."

"Okay. Makes sense."

"Every time I thought we were getting to a place where we could start, something else happened. He got injured. His dreams came back hard. He had that anxiety attack. And so I held off, waiting for us both to be less messed up."

"Did you tell him any of this?"

"Not in so many words. What was I supposed to say? Hey Grady —I think you're too much of a basket case right now to give consent, so I'm holding off for your own good? Like that would have gone over well."

"For what it's worth, I think you've both been train wrecks. You came home with some shit in your head from over there that you haven't laid to rest. I've heard you scream in the middle of the night," Denny said. "And you're not wrong about Grady being in a bad place with Aaron's death. I've been worried about him. So not jumping into a whole new emotional situation probably wasn't a bad idea—but there was likely a better way to go about it."

"Not gonna argue with that. My way obviously wasn't the right one."

"Yeah, well. That's kinda how life works."

"There's something else that I haven't told anyone. I've been afraid that saying it out loud will make it happen, but I swear it's real."

"You're talking about an omen?"

"Yeah. Is what I heard true?"

"Which part? Once you've seen an omen, the danger is already in motion. Talking about it won't bring it on any sooner." Denny fell quiet for a moment. "Something to do with the Black Shuck?"

Dawson nodded, then realized Denny couldn't see him. "Two nights before my unit got ambushed, I dreamed of a big black dog with red eyes." Shucks went by many names in folklore—grim, barghest, even hellhound, like Cunanoon Mountain took its name from. "I couldn't warn anyone. But I took the warning seriously and stayed extra-alert, did what I could. Not that it mattered, in the end."

"You don't know that," Denny said urgently. "Yes, people died. You couldn't control much. But you changed the future by changing your response. It might very well be that's how you lived through it."

"Maybe," Dawson allowed, unconvinced. "I dreamed about the omen again, two weeks before the werewolf attack on Aaron and Grady. I've had it a couple of times since I've been home. And then Grady and I got attacked by one, and he threw himself in front of me to save me and nearly got himself killed."

"And you didn't think it was important enough to tell me this?"

"I didn't want to make anything bad happen." Dawson hated how helpless he felt. "I told myself it was another reason to hold off starting things with Grady because I needed to keep a clear head, keep my focus to protect him. Then I had another dream, Friday night."

"That's a whole lot of omens," Denny observed after he had a moment to think things over. "Has this been a thing for you your whole life, and you never thought to mention it?"

Dawson squirmed. "I've only had it happen a couple of times before. I saw an omen before Mom and Dad were killed. And a few other times. I didn't tell anyone, but I was usually able to change things—go a different route, postpone the hunt, take more weapons. Each time, we got hurt, but nothing really bad."

"You got a theory on why now you're seeing Black Shucks around every corner?"

"Yeah, maybe. Is it possible that Grady and Aaron have an enemy out there looking for revenge?"

Denny went silent for a long time.

"Denny?" Dawson asked.

"I think you might be onto something," Denny replied. "I guess losing Aaron addled my brain. I should have figured it out myself."

Dawson wasn't about to begrudge Denny a lapse while he was grieving his brother. While Aaron might always have felt the need to prove that he was a "real" King, no one else ever felt that way. Denny and Ethan had always loved Aaron as much as if he had been their blood.

"Did they go up against a witch?" Dawson had been turning the idea over in his mind for a couple of days, and he kept coming back to the possibility of a witch bent on vengeance.

"Yeah, they did. A few weeks before Aaron was killed, he and Grady handled a hunt a few towns over where people were dying in odd ways linked to their jobs. A lawyer suffocated when he was buried under an avalanche of paper. An accountant went mad and threw himself off the roof because he couldn't get his checkbook to balance," Denny said.

"Turned out a local witch by the name of Jonathan Kohn felt the people who died had cheated him. No idea whether they actually did —hard to prosecute a dead man."

"What happened when they went after the witch?"

"You know, they were never much for giving the blow-by-blow account after a hunt," Denny grumbled. "From what they did say, the witch put up quite a fight. Aaron and Grady both got their shots in, but they had to work for it."

"Did the witch work alone?" Dawson had the awful feeling that they had stumbled onto the truth.

"If Aaron and Grady knew anything about a second witch or a coven, they didn't tell me. Aaron knows—*knew*—better than to leave a loose end like that. Always comes back to bite you on the ass."

Or the throat.

"Could a witch influence a person's emotions from a distance?"

"You think there's more to it than just Grady grieving for his father?" Denny asked.

Dawson weighed his words before answering. "Maybe. What if the witch kept an eye on Grady when he didn't get killed by the were-wolf? They wouldn't have to cause the feelings—just nudge them to be more extreme. Make everything a little worse."

"It's possible, I guess. But the two of you picked your own hunts these past few weeks. That's pretty hard to blame on the witch."

"I don't think the witch has been trying to get Grady killed on a hunt. I think they wanted him to suffer. Maybe the two witches were friends. Family—or lovers," Dawson suggested.

"So sending Grady over the edge with grief and anxiety—and driving a wedge between him and his true love—are part of the plan?"

Dawson colored at the "true love" comment, then figured he'd best get over it. "Yeah. And sometimes, like with the spirit banishing this morning, it wouldn't take much meddling. The ghost touched Grady, and he saw into her memories."

"You're going to need to tell me more about that at another time," Denny said warily. "I've never heard of such a thing."

"I hadn't, either. But I don't think he just got a glimpse of her memories; I think he picked up on her emotions."

"So he's already grieving, and he's upset because you're back and things between the two of you aren't going the way he'd hoped, or at least not as quickly as he wanted. There's a witch fucking with his emotions, plus a few close calls on hunts, and a dead woman downloads all her angst. Then he thinks he sees the guy he's in love with making googly eyes at someone else. Did I leave anything out?" Denny asked. "Because that sure as shit could push someone over the edge."

"I didn't make googly eyes," Dawson grumbled. "I was trying to get rid of Corbin without tossing him out on his ass and making a scene."

"Next time, throw the son of a bitch through the window so he lands at Grady's feet. It's Neanderthal, but a helluva lot more impressive than flowers."

"There won't be a next time, but I'll keep that in mind," Dawson replied in a dry tone.

"Do you think that this hypothetical witch snatched Grady?"

Dawson was silent for a moment as he thought about it. If Grady had left his things behind, Dawson might have worried that the witch behind the attacks had lured him away, or kidnapped him. But after what Grady had glimpsed—and misunderstood—at the waffle restaurant, coupled with the note, Dawson felt certain this was Grady's choice.

"I don't think he got taken. I think he ran on his own."

They didn't speak for a moment. Finally, Denny broke the silence. "What are you going to do?"

"Find him. I need to fix this. And if we're right, he's in danger. Because the witch wanted to make him suffer—and wants to be the one to kill him."

"Gotta track him down first."

"I called him, left a message, texted. He's not responding."

"Of course not. He's in a snit." Denny let out a long breath. "How long ago did he leave?"

"About forty-five minutes."

"Do you think he'll come home? Either here or to Aaron's house?"

Dawson shook his head. "No. He doesn't want to talk to me. Both of those places are too easy to find him and force a conversation."

"Can you trace his phone?"

"Tried. He must have it powered down. I guess we could try to hack his account or come up with a bullshit story for the cell phone company to get them to do it, but that's gonna take time."

"We could ask Sheriff Rollins to put a trace on it," Denny said.

"And if Grady does end up stealing a car, or breaking and entering to find a place to crash? Rollins would love hauling him in on a charge he could make stick."

"Rollins isn't as much of an asshole as he used to be," Denny replied. "But I get wanting to see if you can find him yourself. Just hope it doesn't take too long. He's angry and alone, and that means he's playing right into the witch's end game."

"That's what I'm afraid of." *And this is just the kind of danger the omen was trying to warn me about.*

"Shit," Denny swore. "He's not real close to most of the rest of the family. Would he go to Knox?"

"Knox isn't exactly who I'd pick for a shoulder to cry on," Dawson replied. Ever since the hunt that sidelined him, Grady's older brother has been stuck in a pretty dark space of his own making.

"Colt?"

Dawson fought down an irrational surge of jealousy. "He never used to be real close to Colt." *Colt was my friend. And sometimes, my friend with benefits. Please tell me he didn't...*

"You're thinking too loudly," Denny said with a wry note in his voice. "I don't think they were ever like that. They did some hunts together while you were gone when Aaron and I were busy. But Colt was always your friend. To be honest, I don't think Grady ever really liked him, after that time the two of you—"

"I remember." And so did Grady, Dawson felt certain. Grady might have trusted Colt enough to hunt beside him, but Colt would be the last person he was likely to turn to for a broken heart—especially when the heartbreaker was Dawson.

"He had a couple of boyfriends at first, after you left. I think you knew that."

"I did." Dawson tried not to remember.

"None of them came around after they broke up, so I don't think he stayed in touch with anyone," Denny mused. "He had some friends from the community college and a few people he hung out with from the garage, but it always sounded casual to me. Not anyone he'd pour his heart out to. I got nothin'."

The ghost of a memory teased Dawson as he tried to recall details from back in high school. "The summer before I left, there was a guy Grady used to play video games with. Not hicky-guy—"

Denny snorted, then cleared his throat. "Sorry."

"Kid had a mop of red hair, looked like he ought to be one of the Weasley brothers—"

"Jimmy," Denny said. "Geez, I'd forgotten all about him. Jimmy McKean. His folks run a sporting goods store."

"Grady went with him and his parents to a cabin one weekend. On a lake, somewhere. Junaluska?"

"No, Lake Toxaway. Grady thought it was really cool because they went fishing from a boat," Denny recalled.

"That's the only place I can think of that doesn't have ties to family," Dawson said. "It's a long shot, but I'm hoping he didn't decide to chuck the whole thing and take off for California or something."

"Grady's a little too old to run away from home," Denny replied. "And I can't imagine him just taking off for good. My bet is that he's hurt and angry, and he overreacted. Of course, if he hitched a ride, he might also come to his senses and realize he's stuck."

"If the witch doesn't find him first." Dawson finally had a plan, and he pinned his phone between his ear and shoulder as he gathered up anything that hadn't been packed that morning.

"Speaking of witches...I think Grady told you that while you were gone, I added some weapons and equipment and useful stuff in the lockbox under Sally's backseat," Denny said.

"Along with keeping the holy water and blessed oil canisters full, I added some charms and amulets and a bunch of dried protective plants and gemstones," Denny went on. "There are two silver, onyx, and agate charms in there—one for each of you—that should help repel dark magic. They won't make you invincible, but they should give you some advantage."

"Thanks," Dawson replied, zipping his bag closed. "I'm going to head to Lake Toxaway. Can you see if you can find an address or a deed for the McLean place? I don't want to lose any more time before I get on the road."

"I'm on it," Denny said. "I hope you're right, Dawson. Go bring him home, and we'll figure out the witch problem."

"That's the plan."

———

THE DRIVE TO LAKE TOXAWAY TOOK LONGER THAN DAWSON HOPED, AND he found himself gritting his teeth and clenching his hands around the Mustang's steering wheel in frustration. His gut knotted with a combination of fear and worry.

What if I get there and he doesn't want to see me? What if he won't believe me about Corbin? If I tell him the whole truth, what will he think?

Dawson tried to just focus on the drive and the music, but his mind spun. *Even if he won't give me a second chance, even if I've totally screwed things up, he needs to know there's a witch after him. I love him. And I'm going to make sure he stays alive—even if I don't get to keep him.*

Normally, Dawson would have enjoyed driving through the mountains, taking in the beautiful landscape. Now, all he could think about was how to stop the witch and maybe...just maybe...work things out with Grady.

Dawson cleared his throat and turned down the radio. Saying what he needed to say wasn't going to be easy. Maybe he needed to practice.

"Grady—I'm sorry. I should have told you the whole truth. I'd been seeing death omens, and I wanted to protect you, needed to keep my head in the game to stop the witch who wants to kill you. And, we've both been so torn up, I didn't want us to start off a relationship when neither one of us were at our best."

Dawson brought one fist down on the wheel in frustration. "Fuck. That's got to be the worst apology in the history of apologies. I suck at this."

For the next half hour, he struggled to come up with the right words. Nothing seemed to work. *If I'd been good at explaining myself, we wouldn't be in this situation.*

"I'm screwed," Dawson admitted to the windshield, saying what he was long overdue to say to Grady. "I've been in love with you since you were seventeen, and I don't want anyone else. Never have. That whole thing I told you about finding yourself? I was just scared you'd wake up someday and realize you could do better than me. And leave. So I didn't take my own advice. I've never done this relationship thing before, and it scares the shit out of me. And I'm fucking it all up, and I don't know how to fix it."

Honest, but bordering on pathetic.

Before he could launch into another version of his apology, his phone rang with Denny's ringtone. "I just texted you the address. You should be able to get directions from that. From what I could find out online, the lake has a lot of summer cabins, but there's plenty of room between them, very private. Perfect place for an ambush."

He paused. "Just in case, I'm going to check Aaron's house and see if anyone from the shop has seen him. And I'll send Colt to touch base at the community college. It can't hurt."

"Thanks, Denny. I'll call when I know more."

"Damn well better. I'm not getting any younger, and you two don't help my blood pressure." He paused. "Good luck. With all of it."

Denny ended the call, leaving Dawson alone once more. He knew he needed to get his head together about how to fight the witch because if that went wrong, he wouldn't have a chance to apologize.

Whoever the witch is, they've got to be keeping an eye on Grady. If there's a spell on him, maybe that creates a link the witch can use to know what he's doing. Does the witch know about me? Did they factor me into the plan somehow, or am I a dark horse?

His phone rang again a while later. "Yeah, Denny?"

"I've got a name, I think, for the second witch. Paul Franco. Grady and Aaron didn't just kill his partner in magic. Paul and Jonathan were married."

"Fuck."

"Be careful, Dawson. If this witch wants revenge, you've got as big a target on your back as Grady does."

For the last half of the drive, Dawson and Denny debated how best to ward against the witch and his dark magic, or if push came to shove, how to fight back.

"I can't do magic," Dawson protested. "Maybe the omens I saw were a little paranormal, but that's not the same. If Franco is really keeping an eye on Grady somehow, then it's going to be hard to take him by surprise."

"Except that he doesn't *know* you know."

Dawson thought about it and nodded. "Okay, it's not much, but I'll take it. So I go walking in looking like an easy mark, and he gets more than he bargained for?"

"It's the best we've got," Denny replied. "You should have everything you need in the compartment under the seat. Make sure you use the charms. Don't try to be fancy. Use the brass bullets—they're more effective on witches. There's a brass knife as well, and a mistletoe stake. You're a good hunter. You can do this."

I have to do this for Grady. And maybe, if I'm lucky, for a second chance.

———

DAWSON PULLED OVER AT AN ABANDONED GAS STATION TO GET THE items from beneath the Mustang's back seat. He wore one set of the witch charms, which dangled from a leather strap that he slipped over his head. The second set he put in his pocket for Grady. Then he loaded his gun, grabbed a stake, and clipped the brass knife's sheath to his belt. Dawson slid the gun and the stake underneath the driver's seat, pulled up the address Denny sent him on his phone GPS and hoped he wasn't too late.

He made good time. Dawson pushed the speed limit to arrive before twelve, since both noon and midnight were times associated with stronger magic. The witch had enough advantages; he didn't need to gain any more.

The cabins were directly on the lake, with long, winding driveways. Dawson drove down the quiet, tree-lined road that circled the lake searching for the right address, acutely aware of the Mustang's rumble, a sound he usually loved. Not only would it be a dead giveaway to Grady that he was coming, but the witch would have no difficulty pinpointing his location.

About halfway down the driveway to the house, Dawson pulled onto the manicured grass and shut off the car. He reached for the gun beneath his seat and slipped it into the waistband of his jeans. The stake, made from rowan wood sharpened and soaked in a mistletoe potion, fit into a pocket inside his jacket. Other pockets held a variety of handy objects, just in case.

Dawson crept along the inside of the row of trees that lined the driveway. As he got closer, he could see the house. A rustic cabin sat on a rise overlooking the lake. The cabin had a wrap-around porch and a large mowed yard, more a vacation home than a basic hunting cabin. From here, he could glimpse the lake, where the bright sun made the water glisten.

If Grady had heard the Mustang, it hadn't drawn him to the balcony. Dawson kept a sharp eye out for the witch, but saw no one as he approached.

Maybe he could get Grady to leave with him, and they could sort things out back at Denny's house, where wardings and other protections gave them a better chance against Franco. But Dawson doubted that Grady was likely to leave without clearing the air, which would be loud and not particularly quick. They'd both be at risk of being ambushed by the witch while they argued.

If Dawson could chalk sigils to protect against dark magic around the outside of the cabin, it would keep them safe from an ambush. He had painted the same symbols inside the hood, trunk, and door panels of the Mustang long ago. Both the paint and the chalk used a combination of ingredients that amplified the power of the sigils themselves. Franco wouldn't be able to cross the marks.

Of course, that meant Dawson had to cover the stretch of open ground to get to the house. He wondered if Grady had been thinking clearly enough to ward the house, or if he had been too preoccupied to do more than seek shelter.

One thing was certain—the lot sat far enough away from any neighbors that no one was likely to hear or see what went on, short of sending up fireworks. Dawson wasn't sure whether that was good or bad.

He crouched in the shadows between two trees, making a last sweep of the approach. If he sprinted, he could be across the yard in seconds. The wooden porch supports would be perfect places to chalk the sigils, and after he and Grady left, the marks would likely be attributed to teenage vandalism. Dawson didn't care as long as he and Grady were together and alive.

Dawson took off running. A glowing, green fog appeared out of nowhere blocking his path. It smelled of ash and sulfur. He veered to the side. The fog matched his move. When he tried to zig-zag, the fog tracked his course, interposing itself between Dawson and the cabin.

The green cloud suddenly changed direction and expanded, engulfing Dawson despite his efforts to avoid it. A chill settled over him, and the magic of the cloud stole his breath, sending him to his knees.

"Dawson King. I've been waiting for you."

Paul Franco looked to be in his mid-thirties, with a shaved head, brown beard, and piercing dark eyes. There was no mistaking the cold hatred in his gaze, or the malice in the man's slight smile.

Dawson reached up to wrap his hand around the amulets, and the effects of the fog lessened. He could get his breath, and the paralyzing cold receded.

"Interesting." Franco gestured, and the fog thickened again. The glow shifted and changed, and images emerged. Whether Franco could somehow read memories or knew enough to make a good guess, Dawson didn't know, but as he focused on claiming the amulets' protection, the images grew clearer. He saw battlefields like those he had served on, heard the scream of planes and the blast of bombs.

Dawson bit his tongue, drawing on his will to keep the sights and sounds from affecting him.

Franco chuckled. "Once you've seen true horrors, they never leave you," he said, his voice smooth and mocking. "Losing your comrades on the field of war. Seeing your lover cut down in cold blood...it's not something you ever forget."

"Jonathan wasn't an innocent," Dawson managed through gritted teeth. He moved his right hand slowly toward the gun in his waistband. "He'd been murdering people he didn't like. Did you help him?"

Franco's eyes narrowed. "They had it coming. We weren't the first people they victimized. But we were the last."

"You could have turned them in to the police."

Franco's laugh sent ice down Dawson's spine. "The police didn't listen to the others; they wouldn't have listened to us. The way I see it, we provided a public service."

"You get to decide who lives and who dies?"

"Like hunters?"

"We kill monsters. Monsters like you." Dawson nearly had a grip on his gun.

"Your cousin killed the man I loved. I intend to return the favor before I take his life as recompense."

Dawson grabbed his gun, rolled, and came up shooting. Franco staggered as one bullet caught him in the shoulder, but then the green fog vanished, and an invisible force knocked Dawson off his feet, throwing him to one side and ripping the gun from his grasp.

Blood darkened the side of Franco's jacket, and pain tightened his mouth, but it didn't blunt his magic. Dawson wondered whether the witch had intended to survive the encounter, or whether he meant to get his revenge and then join his lover.

"Not so easy, hunter." Franco saw Dawson reach for his gun and flipped the weapon farther away while sending him tumbling in the other direction.

Dawson hugged his arms to his chest to make sure the stake didn't slide free. He dared not loosen his grip on the amulets since they had helped with the fog. Given all the things Franco could do to him, Dawson didn't want to see what might happen without the charms' protection.

Their fight had moved them closer to the house, although it was still some yards away. Dawson hadn't seen motion at the windows, or anything to confirm his guess that Grady had taken shelter here. Yet Franco had been tracking him, so Grady must be nearby. How the hell did he not realize there was a fight outside his window?

In the next breath, Dawson hoped against hope that Grady had gone elsewhere. Franco clearly meant to kill them both. Dawson might not escape, but if Grady wasn't here, at least he would survive.

His gun had vanished in the grass, but Dawson pulled his brass knife and flung it, aimed for Franco's heart.

Franco brought one hand up, and the knife stilled in mid-air, then slowly turned and flew back at Dawson, slicing through his left upper arm. Dawson didn't doubt that if Franco had wanted him dead, the knife would be hilt-deep in his chest. The witch meant to draw out and savor the encounter.

"Enough of that." Franco closed his hand, and Dawson felt dragged by an invisible chain, scrambling to keep from being strangled.

"Much better," Franco said, at the sight of Dawson on his hands and knees.

Taking advantage of where he was, Dawson spit on the witch's expensive leather shoes.

"Time to end this." Franco reached down and grabbed Dawson by the throat, then lifted him to dangle at arm's length, his strength aided by magic.

Of all the ways Dawson ever thought he might die, being Force-choked wasn't one of them.

Dawson kicked and twisted, but Franco's magic kept him from doing any damage to the witch. He still had the stake in his jacket, but while the witch watched him closely, there was no chance to draw it without it being snatched away.

"Grady King! I know you're in there," Franco's voice boomed as if the strain of holding a grown man aloft didn't faze him. "Come watch while I kill your lover before I finish you."

Dawson didn't think Grady intended to answer, and then one of the glass doors slid open hard enough to rattle. Grady stumbled out, a half-empty whiskey bottle gripped by the neck in his left hand, and his Sig Sauer in his right.

"He's not my lover," Grady slurred. "You know what? I'm mad at him." He waved the gun in the air, aiming mostly at the sky as he staggered toward the railing. "Got half a mind to shoot him myself."

Franco tightened his hold. Dawson struggled to breathe, wondering whether the witch would be content to just crush his windpipe or let him slowly strangle. Pinpricks of light and dark spots danced in his vision as he tried to rip away Franco's hand or kick him in the nuts. Neither worked.

"My mistake. I thought his death would hurt you—as the murder of my Jonathan hurt me."

"Oh, now there you've got it all wrong." Grady nearly tripped, but he righted himself at the railing. "See, we didn't murder anyone. He had it coming, man. Stone-cold killer, that fucker was. I got no regrets about capping him. None at all."

For the love of God, Gray, shut the fuck up! It wasn't like Grady to say things like that, but then Dawson was coming to realize that their four years apart meant he didn't know this version of Grady as well as he thought he had. Pity he wouldn't live long enough to learn more.

"Lies! All lies! Jonathan wasn't like that." Dawson saw the rage building on Franco's face.

Grady wobbled, smiling lopsidedly. "He wasn't even that good of a witch." Grady took another swig from the bottle, still pointing the gun at the sky, although it swayed back and forth alarmingly. "I mean, two hunters with no magic took him down. What kind of witch would let that happen?"

"Jonathan trained for years! He knew the old grimoires. How dare you insult him like that!"

Keep him monologuing, Dawson thought as he dragged in a ragged breath. *Villains always lose when they monologue.* He felt Franco's grip ease, just a bit. It was enough to let him draw a full breath.

"You know what I think?" Grady swayed toward the rail like he might pitch over it headfirst. "I think you're a fake. Jonathan was a fake witch, and you're a fake witch, and Daw's a fake boyfriend." He raised the bottle. "You know what isn't fake? This whiskey. It's good scotch." The "s" sounds became "sh," and Dawson wondered how much Grady could have downed in a little over an hour to get quite so wasted.

"I assure you, I'm the real thing. Let me demonstrate." Franco turned back to Dawson and tightened his grip. Dawson saw his death reflected in the witch's eyes.

The bang of a gunshot sounded loud enough to send birds aloft from the trees behind them.

Fuck. Gray's drunk and shooting. We're all gonna die.

Franco jerked, eyes widening as a crimson stain colored the

center of his shirt. The witch's hold eased just enough for Dawson to jerk the stake from his coat and plunge it into Franco's ribs.

The witch's hand went slack, dropping Dawson on his ass as Franco's body slumped to the ground.

Dawson rubbed his neck; sure he'd have bruises tomorrow, still trying to believe he had survived.

Gray. I've got to get to Gray. He looked up at the deck. Grady was gone.

10

GRADY

GRADY SET THE BOTTLE ON THE TABLE, ALONG WITH HIS GUN. HIS hands shook, and he wanted to throw up.

It didn't surprise him in the least when Dawson came in over the porch railing, rather than going around to the door.

"What the fuck, Gray?" Dawson demanded, as he stripped off his jacket and tossed it over a chair. "You could have shot me!"

Grady glared at him. "Who says I wasn't trying to?"

He dropped the fake drunk act, and the slurred speech he'd added for effect. *Damn fine performance, if I do say so myself.*

The house had a well-stocked liquor cabinet, and Grady had availed himself of the top-shelf bounty. But since he figured he had all day to drink away a broken heart, he had been trying to pace himself. So he was rocking a good buzz, which had almost been wiped away by the pure terror of seeing Dawson in Franco's grip.

"You're not really drunk."

Grady rounded on him. "Oh, I was getting there. Just had a little interruption."

Dawson stalked towards him. "You left!"

Grady swung a punch, and Dawson blocked it, barely. Grady

didn't put his full strength into the blow, just wanting to send a message. Dawson staggered back a step, eyes wide.

"What did you expect me to do? Make it a threesome?" The pain and anger rushed back, meaning Grady hadn't had nearly enough whiskey to make it go away.

Dawson rushed him and pinned him to the wall, strong hands gripping his wrists, lower half held in place by the weight of Dawson's body pressing against him.

"Did you listen to the damn phone message? I told him to leave. Told him I wasn't on the market anymore. I told him I had a fucking boyfriend, for chrissake!"

Dawson's face was just inches from his own. Grady could smell the mix of sweat, shaving cream, and soap that had always been Dawson. Dawson's dark eyes looked frantic, and underneath his anger, Grady saw the fear.

"A fucking boyfriend you haven't fucked? How's that work, Daw?"

"Gray, it's not liked that."

"Yeah? How is it then? Been home ten weeks already. Were you ever going to get around to it?" Grady shoved hard, managing to flip them around, so he was the one pinning Dawson. He closed his hands around Dawson's wrists, giving him a taste of his own medicine.

Dawson's eyes widened a fraction, pupils dilating. His breath came shallow and fast, color rising to his cheeks. Grady shoved his knee between Dawson's legs and ground against him. His cock had been hard from the moment Dawson pushed him against the wall. From the stiff length Grady could feel through Dawson's jeans, they were finally on the same page.

"I saw omens, Gray. Black Shucks. Before I got shot in Afghanistan. Before Aaron died. Then I got home, and you were grieving, and I was messed up, and I kept dreaming about those damn black dogs. And I thought you were going to die, Gray. I didn't want to pressure you, and I didn't want to drag you into my mess. And I was afraid something was trying to kill you. I had to save you, Gray. I had to."

Dawson's words spilled out, fast and desperate. Grady could hear the truth of them. That didn't mean he was ready to forgive, although his aching cock definitely argued for leniency. Or maybe in favor of making Dawson work for his reprieve.

"We promised each other, Daw. I thought you wanted this as much as I do."

"Gray, please. I do want you. So bad, for so long. I had all these plans for when I got back, wanted to sweep you off your feet, do this right." The raw, husky tone beneath Dawson's pleading words made heat coil in Grady's belly.

"And then, you were hurt, Gray. I wanted to hold you, take the pain away, make you forget. But I was afraid. Didn't want to take advantage, or make you feel pressured. Waited so long to get this right, babe. And then I fucked it all up anyhow."

"I wanted you next to me, keeping the dreams away," Grady confessed, dropping his voice low so it only carried the inches between them. "I wanted to be in your bed when your nightmares came, be there for you."

Dawson pushed away from the wall hard enough to carry them both to the floor. He landed on top of Grady, knees straddling Grady's hips, pinning his wrists above his head. The brown of his eyes was a thin ring around dark pupils blown wide.

Grady felt his pulse speed as Dawson's body pressed against him, holding him down, cocks rubbing together in almost painful arousal.

"You scared me." Dawson's voice was deeper than Grady had ever heard it. It sounded like his wet dreams, like he imagined Daw might talk to someone lucky enough to be in his bed.

"You ran, and I came after you. But there were old people blocking the door, and then those fucking trucks...and you were gone. I didn't know what to do, Gray. And then I found out the witch had been messing with your head, making everything worse, and I lost it. I should have told you everything, should have come right out and said how much I wanted you. I've never done this before, Gray. I don't know how to not screw up."

Grady couldn't fight a bitter laugh. "Never done what, Daw? You think I didn't know what you and Colt were up to in the barn? Do you know how long I hated him because he got to touch you and I didn't? And those trips to Asheville? I knew. And I couldn't figure out what I was doing wrong that you wanted them and not me."

"For one thing, you were jailbait." Dawson drew a long breath. "And none of those were relationships. None of them mattered."

Grady wasn't quite over his temper. "That guy, this morning—he was one of your hookups, wasn't he?"

Dawson looked away. "Yeah."

"He looked a lot like me."

Dawson turned back, fixing Grady with a scorching look. "They all did, Gray. All of them. Because I didn't want them—I wanted you, and I couldn't have you."

Grady was panting, and his heart felt like it would beat out of his chest. Dawson shifted, sparking heat where their erections rubbed together. The thick area rug cushioned them from the floor, and Grady hoped he'd have rug burn to remember this by.

"So what's stopping you now?" He arched up, increasing the friction between them, and Dawson groaned.

Dawson released one of Grady's wrists, but Grady didn't move. One hand cupped Grady's face, fingers gentle on his skin, the pad of his thumb skimming across Grady's slightly parted lips.

"You're it for me, Gray. If we do this, it's not a hookup or a fling. It's forever. If you don't want that, tell me now."

"I want that. I want you." He bucked up, seeking that beautiful friction again. "Now will you fuck me already?"

"Where?"

Grady just stared at him. "Mouth or ass are the usual choices."

Dawson gave him a slow blink. "I meant, do you want to do it on the floor, bent over the coffee table, on your knees on the couch, spread-eagle in a bed, or on top of the table, dipshit."

"All of the above."

Dawson swallowed hard, but Grady felt sure it had more to do with arousal than impatience. "Then get naked. That's a lot of territory to cover."

Dawson moved off Grady's hips, and Grady watched as he stripped off his T-shirt and tossed it aside. Dawson had a leaner build, but still strong and defined. Tawny nipples stood out against his skin, and a trail of dark hair led down below his belt. Two new pink scars marked where the bullet and shrapnel had hit, the wounds that had almost killed Dawson in Afghanistan.

Grady had stolen glances at Dawson all his life, careful not to be too obvious. Realizing he could look and touch as much as he wanted almost made him cream his jeans.

"If you're gonna look at me while I strip, you'd better have some bills to stick in my waistband," Dawson snarked.

"I've got something else to stick there. Keep going."

Dawson grinned, and Grady thought that despite Dawson looking a bit self-conscious, he seemed to like Grady's attention, gauging from the bulge at his crotch. Dawson stood and shot him a wicked grin as he unbuckled his belt, then unzipped his jeans. He pushed his jeans and his boxer-briefs down in one move, then toed out of shoes and socks.

From his vantage point on the floor, Grady had a good view of Dawson's heavy balls and the stiff, reddened cock that slapped against his belly, already leaking pre-come. Grady met Dawson's gaze and licked his lips.

"You're wearing too much clothing," Dawson said, which didn't hide the way his face pinked at Grady's unabashed appreciation.

"I can fix that." Grady rose to his knees and quickly shed his T-shirt. He didn't miss how Dawson's gaze immediately found the mostly-healed gashes from the werewolf and the old scars from the long-ago wendigo. Not wanting the past to ruin the mood, Grady stood and made a move for his belt.

"Let me." Dawson closed the space between them, almost chest to chest. He ran his knuckles gently along Grady's chin, and Grady leaned into the gesture. Then Dawson's lips met his, and Grady's brain fuzzed out for a second at the sensation and the realization that this was finally, *finally* happening.

Dawson's tongue flicked across Grady's lips, and Grady opened his mouth, letting Dawson claim him. Dawson's hand slipped around to the back of Grady's head, angling him to deepen the kiss, but not gripping so tightly that Grady couldn't have broken the hold if he wanted to.

Grady moaned, and brought his arms up behind Dawson, splaying his hands on the taut muscles and smooth skin of his naked back. In all the years when Grady had fantasized about kissing Dawson, the reality was so much better. Dawson's lips, full and soft, took Grady's breath away. He'd always secretly thought lips like that were made for cock-sucking, and jerked off many a night to the thought of them wrapped around his dick. Knowing that was likely to actually happen almost made him spurt like a teenager.

"What do you want?" Dawson murmured next to Grady's ear, in a voice that sounded like sin and whiskey.

"Everything."

Dawson chuckled, a low, rumbling sound that went straight to Grady's balls. "That can be arranged. Let's get you naked. May I?" His hand slipped down from where he claimed Grady's hip to tug gently at his buckle.

"God, yes!" Grady managed, still feeling a bit scrambled now that his secret fantasies were unfolding in real life.

Dawson paused for a moment. "Just so you know, I'm negative. Army tested us regularly. Haven't been with anyone in almost two years."

"Me, too. Negative. There hasn't been anyone in a very long time."

Dawson never stopped kissing Grady as his hand moved to unfasten the buckle and open the zipper. He let the jeans fall, and then his hand palmed Grady's ass through his boxer-briefs, giving a firm squeeze.

"Love your ass," he growled as he gently nipped and kissed along Grady's jaw. Grady felt a brush of stubble as Dawson nuzzled higher, tongue tracing the sensitive shell of Grady's ear, and he shivered.

"Keep that up, and I won't last," Grady warned, losing himself in the sensation.

"Go ahead. I'll just make you come again."

Dawson's hand slipped to the front to palm Grady's cock, and his thumb ran over the sensitive head, where the cloth was damp.

"There are so many things I've wanted to do with you." His voice was a sexy growl, even better than Grady had ever imagined. "I used to feel so guilty, imagining me sucking your cock, or you on your knees, sucking me. But it was always you, Gray. Always."

Dawson bent to kiss Grady's neck, and Grady canted his head, baring his throat. He gasped as Dawson sucked a hickey into the flesh where his neck and shoulder met.

"Mine," he whispered.

"Always yours," Grady replied, afraid he might wake up to find it all a cruel hallucination.

Dawson's hands gripped him by the waist as his lips moved from one hard pink nub to the other, licking and sucking until they pebbled. Grady bowed backward, offering himself, trusting Dawson to hold onto him.

Lips and tongue worked their way past his navel, then down his happy trail to the waistband of Grady's boxer-briefs.

Grady expected Dawson to peel them off, but instead, he wrapped his mouth against Grady's leaking bulge and exhaled as his tongue swept over the wet fabric, tasting him and enveloping him in warm heat.

"You're killing me," Grady groaned.

Dawson's chuckle made no apologies. "We're just getting started," he replied, making sure Grady felt every movement of his lips on his rigid, overly sensitive cock.

Grady squirmed, and Dawson dropped his hands to hold his hips steady, firm enough that Grady hoped he would have finger-print bruises tomorrow, proof that he hadn't imagined the whole thing.

"Daw—"

"Gonna take real good care of you," Dawson said, in a voice so full of emotion it made Grady's heart clench.

Dawson snagged the waistband in his teeth and tugged, inching them down. He paused to bury his face against Grady's groin, taking in his scent, something so primal and claiming that Grady had to bite back a moan.

One hand loosened its grip on his hipbone long enough to push the barrier down, and Grady shook off his jeans and underwear, leaving him completely naked.

"So beautiful," Dawson said, almost to himself, letting his hand run through the fine blond hair on Grady's thigh, feeling his muscles tremble, before rising to his hip once more.

He kissed and licked at the seam of Grady's groin, then ignored Grady's desperate moan as he moved around his weeping cock to go lower, nosing at heavy balls before taking one and then the other into his mouth, rolling them on his tongue, tugging to wring a new sound from Grady's throat.

"Please," Grady moaned, not too proud to beg.

Dawson's answer was to swallow him down to the root, while one hand cupped his balls, and the other held him firmly by the hip.

"Oh, God; oh, God; oh, God," Grady chanted as Dawson took him deep enough to bump the back of his throat, then bobbed up to the head, swirling his tongue around the top and drawing the tip through that oh-so-sensitive slit before hollowing his cheeks and doing it all again.

Grady looked down and nearly lost it right then, watching Dawson sucking his cock. Then those brown eyes looked up at him, meeting his gaze beneath long lashes, and Grady knew it was over.

"Daw, I'm gonna—"

Dawson gave one more long lick up his shaft, and Grady came with a shout, needing his lover's hands on his hips to keep his knees from buckling with the force of his climax. He pumped his load down Dawson's willing throat, and Dawson took it all, swallowing him down, then carefully licking him clean to get every drop.

Grady slumped to his knees, with Dawson controlling his fall, then taking him in his arms. "Was that okay?" Dawson teased and kissed Grady so he could taste himself on those same plump lips.

"Way better than okay." Grady regained the presence of mind to remember to return the favor. He ran his fingers down Dawson's chest and watched him shiver at the touch. Grady only spared a moment to tweak each of those dark peaks to hardness before letting his hand trail farther, gently brushing over the bullet scar, then on down until he wrapped around Dawson's hot, very hard cock. The sight of it made his spent dick twitch, already wanting another round.

"Gray," Dawson murmured, "touch me."

Dawson leaned back, still on his knees, arms stretched out behind him, legs spread, exposing his muscular body. Enough pre-come slicked Grady's hand that it only took a few long pulls to stroke his cock and send Dawson's release fountaining over his fingers. White ropes of come spattered Dawson's chest, and a few droplets hit his chin. Grady worked him through it until his cock softened, and Dawson moaned from his touch on too-sensitive flesh.

Dawson's arms buckled, and he dropped back to the floor, unfolding his legs to stretch them out, looking sated and debauched. Grady took in the sight for a moment, committing it to memory, lost in the scent and taste, the realization that *he had just jerked Dawson off.* Then he got an idea and rose on his knees, planting one hand on either side of Dawson's prone form before he began licking the come off his body, lapping it up like cream.

He cleaned the last droplets from Dawson's chin, then pressed a kiss to his lips, sharing some of the bounty. Dawson's arms came up around him, pulling Grady to his chest. Grady could smell a mixture of Dawson's spend and his own spit, and their mingled sweat. He'd never known a more seductive fragrance.

They lay in silence for a while, comfortable on the thick area rug. Grady listened to the steady thump of Dawson's heart. Dawson's fingers combed through Grady's hair as if the silky curls fascinated him.

"Did you break in?" Dawson asked after a long pause. Grady looked up at him since that was the last thing he'd expected.

"What?"

"I know your friend's parents own the place. Did you break in?"

"I don't think we have to worry about the cops showing up. Why?"

Dawson pushed a stray lock of hair out of Grady's eyes. "Because I want to take you to bed, Gray. I want to make love to you. And it's just wrong to think of doing that in a stolen bed when we can't even wash the sheets."

"Think of the DNA evidence," Grady quipped. "Blacklight reveals all."

Dawson gently smacked him on the side of the head. "Be serious."

Grady chuckled. "I love that you want to make an honest man of me," he replied, and the sentiment behind Dawson's question did mean a lot. It drove home his earlier vow, that this wasn't a one-night stand, a convenient way to scratch an itch. Not that a hot fast fuck up against the wall couldn't be sexy as hell on occasion, but it wasn't the way to start things off with the love of your life.

"I stayed in touch with Jimmy—just as a friend—online," Grady replied. "We played some of the same video games. I still had his phone number. So when I didn't know where else to go, I remembered this cabin from that summer we visited. I called him, fudged the details, and asked if I could hide out here for a little bit and get my head together. He told me where to find the key and how to turn off the alarm. Just asked me to run the towels and sheets through the wash, take out the trash, restock anything I ate—normal clean-up stuff."

"For how long?" Dawson's lazy smile promised all kinds of carnal pleasures.

Grady smiled right back, hoping Dawson could read all the things he was feeling. "His parents are in Europe for the next couple of months, and he didn't have any plans to use it. So we can stay as long as we want."

"Hmm," Dawson replied, and Grady felt the vibration. "We'd have the place all to ourselves, a bed—"

"A California king-size bed," Grady interrupted.

"Even better. I imagine there's a grocery store somewhere we could buy whatever they don't keep on hand. Nice liquor cabinet."

"There's a great view from the deck on the other side," Grady pointed out. "The hot tub isn't set up, but the master bath has a Jacuzzi big enough for two."

"I suppose we could find trails to hike."

"If we ever leave the bedroom."

"Making up for lost time?" Dawson asked, running his fingertips through Grady's hair and across his scalp. Grady closed his eyes and pushed into the motion. He'd always had a thing for someone touching his hair. Pulling a little, too, in the right circumstances. Dawson would figure that out for himself, fairly soon.

"You know it."

"We can pick up lube and condoms when we get groceries."

Grady couldn't help blushing. "Uh, we don't need to. I mean, we're both negative, and I trust you, so if you trust me—"

"You know I do."

"Then we don't need the condoms. And I have lube in my duffel."

Dawson shifted to look at him and raised an eyebrow. "Oh, really?"

Grady felt the heat rise. "I was very...hopeful. Been carrying it around with me since you got home. Just in case."

He felt Dawson's calloused palm gently cup his face again, something he felt certain would never get old. Grady splayed his hand on Dawson's chest, over his heart. Dawson turned Grady's head to meet his gaze. He thought those brown eyes had never been more beautiful.

"You know I love you, Grady King," Dawson said, his voice dropping low enough to make Grady's cock twitch with renewed interest.

"Love you too, Dawson King," Grady replied, marveling at the emotions he saw mirrored in his lover's eyes. "Always have, always will." He couldn't resist smirking. "And just think—neither one of us has to change his last name."

Dawson chuckled. "We could always hyphenate."

"People will think we stuttered."

"Saves on needing to get new monograms."

"Neither of us own anything with a monogram," Grady pointed out, loving the way the easy banter had returned. Mind-blowing orgasms really were the best way to work off tension.

"Well then, we've got it all taken care of."

Grady snuggled back against Dawson, finding that he fit just perfectly into the spot between chest and shoulder. Dawson closed his arms around him, pulling them close together, protective and promising.

After a little while, Grady wriggled out of Dawson's embrace. Dawson looked puzzled, and Grady did his best to answer with what he hoped was a lascivious grin. He reached down and tugged Dawson's wrist.

"Bed."

Dawson chuckled. "In a hurry?"

"Been waiting too damn long to be patient," Grady replied as Dawson got to his feet. Dawson wrapped an arm around him, drawing him close, so they molded together from knees to lips. Grady let his hand slip down to palm Dawson's perfect ass.

"Lead the way," Dawson murmured. "And don't forget the lube."

Grady had never been assertive with his few past lovers. Those had been fumbling encounters, figuring out how to maneuver, awkward and not especially satisfying. Still, Grady's heart pounded so fast that he couldn't imagine what it would have been like to have gotten his teenage fantasies granted, and to be finally going to bed with Dawson without having any experience with sex at all.

I'd have fainted, probably knocked myself out, and been my own cock-blocker.

The cabin's master bedroom was rustic, masculine, and comfortable. A braided rug covered part of the pine floor. The fireplace looked inviting and functional, with two oversized chairs in front for lounging. The blue and green tones of the comforter, pillow shams, and curtains fit with the scenery on the other side of the large French doors. Colorful plaid throw pillows and accents lent an added punch.

Grady grabbed the top edge of the comforter and yanked it back, baring the sheets beneath. Before he could do anything else, Dawson took him in his arms again and kissed him with so much heat Grady wasn't sure he'd last to the main event.

"How do you like it?" Dawson asked in that sexy growl that already had Grady chubbing up again.

"Um," Grady felt his cheeks heat.

Dawson pulled back far enough to look him in the eye. "Gray... have you ever done this before?"

Oh, shit. Did I do something to give off virgin vibes? Sexiness fled, and mortification moved in.

"Yes. Of course. Sort of."

Dawson pulled him down onto the bed, tossing the lube to one side. He turned them so they faced each other, and for a few moments, he didn't speak, appreciating Grady's naked body with his gaze and letting his hands graze over his skin in a way that felt more like worship than seduction.

"Sort of?"

The last thing Grady wanted to talk about were his past encounters. "I've never gone all the way," he admitted, then wanted to facepalm. *Gone all the way? What is this, high school? Just shoot me now.*

He cleared his throat, hurrying before Dawson could say anything. "I mean, I haven't bottomed. Or topped, either. I was, um, waiting."

A fire lit in Dawson's eyes, reminding Grady of a hungry wolf—in the best possible way. "What do you mean, 'waiting'?"

Grady let his gaze fall. "For you. I kept hoping that if I got a little experience, you would want me as a lover, but I never met anyone I trusted enough to actually have real sex with, and I kept hoping it would be you, so...yeah."

Dawson tipped Grady's chin up, and Grady reluctantly met his gaze. "First off, it all counts as 'real sex.' There isn't one way or position that's more 'real' than anything else. Some people do everything. Some only do it a few ways, ever. Still real. And still good. Intimate."

"Okay." Grady couldn't help feeling mortified.

"Second, you never had to earn my attention, Gray. I've wanted you for a lover since you were legal." He reached out to brush the hair from Grady's eyes and stroke his fingers down his cheek.

"And third, it is unbelievably hot that you waited for me. I didn't expect it. I hated the guy I thought you lost it to, honestly. But you don't know how many times I imagined what it would be like to be your first."

Between the heat in Dawson's gaze and the husky growl of his voice, Grady thought he might come before they even got started. He couldn't avoid noticing that Dawson had gotten hard again.

"Really?"

Dawson's dirty chuckle went right to Grady's cock. "Believe it." His hand slid down Grady's shoulder and arm, then down his side to the dip of his waist and the rise of his hip. Grady could smell the scent of their arousal, and he had never been so turned on in his life.

"You had a blue V-neck shirt that fit snug, and a pair of jeans that were so tight, I knew which way you were hung."

Grady swallowed hard. "I remember," he whispered. *I wore them to get to you. Holy hell, you noticed.*

"That was one of my favorite outfits of yours. I couldn't take my eyes off you. I was afraid you'd catch me looking."

Grady shook his head. "I didn't—but I wanted you to."

Dawson let his finger lazily trace circles on Grady's belly, around his navel, through the blond hair scattered over his chest, and up and around his hard nubs. Grady reached out tentatively, too wrapped up in what Dawson was saying to concentrate on touching.

"Oh, I did. I took a lot of cold showers because of those jeans," Dawson confessed. "And when I was alone, I'd think about peeling off that T-shirt, licking my way down your chest, and then working those tight jeans off your ass. You had to have been commando underneath—"

"I was."

Dawson groaned. "I knew it. And I thought of every way I could make you come. Wanted to see you give it up for me."

"Daw—"

"And I thought about what it would feel like to open you up, nice and slow, teach you how good it can feel hitting that perfect spot, rim you until you begged for it, and then make you come on my cock."

Dawson reached down and let his fingers trace ever so gently up Grady's painfully hard erection. "In my mind, I put you up against the wall in the barn, bent over and legs wide, so I could reach around and jack you at the same time. Wanted to sneak off to that pretty little place by the lake and do you there, on your hands and knees." He slipped his hand behind Grady's cock, fondling his balls, and Grady gasped.

"Or I thought about driving us out to that overlook where you can see the stars over the mountain and getting you to ride me in the front seat of the Mustang. Imagining what you'd look like in the moonlight, sinking down on my cock—"

"God, Daw—less talking. I want you. Want this. Now. Please."

"Gonna make sure this is good for you, Gray," Dawson promised, leaning forward to kiss him gently. "First time's going to be easier from behind, but after you get used to me, there are other ways we can try."

He cupped Grady's ass. "Get on your knees for me, Gray."

Grady scrambled to comply. He pinched himself, just to make sure this was all real. Because it was just the way he'd always hoped it would be—only better.

11

DAWSON

FOR SO LONG, DAWSON HAD WONDERED WHAT IT WOULD BE LIKE TO have the real Grady in his bed as a lover. Not fantasy-Grady, who was plenty hot, but just a wet dream. But the real man, stubborn, sassy, serious, and intense.

He couldn't believe this was really happening, not even when Grady flipped over, getting his knees under him, leaning forward on his forearms, offering up his ass.

His *virgin* ass. The intimacy he'd saved for Dawson, hoping that someday those dreams would become real.

Dawson reached down and squeezed the root of his cock to keep this from being over before it even began. He slipped a pillow beneath his lover to make the position easier. Then he knelt over Grady, his knees nudging Grady's legs wider, and bent forward to kiss down the ridge of his spine, then licked into the dimples on either side at the base.

"Daw—" The desperate hunger in Grady's voice made Dawson's balls draw up.

"Soon," he murmured. "Need to make this good. Not going to hurt you."

He knew this first time wouldn't set endurance records for either of them. Dawson's hands shook, and he felt far more nervous than he had when he'd lost his own virginity. But he remembered clearly how much it hurt without the right prep. He swore he'd make sure Grady never experienced that.

Dawson kissed his way down farther, then parted Grady's ass cheeks and licked down his crack, pausing to tease that sensitive hole with the tip of his tongue, before descending to an equally sensitive taint.

"Fuck. Daw—"

He worked his way back up, working the tight pucker with his tongue, feeling Grady tremble from his touch. Dawson thought he might shoot off just from the noises Grady made. He reached for the lube and coated a finger, then pressed into the spit-slick hole, moving slowly. Grady's muscles clamped around him, so tight and hot.

"Not going to hurt you, babe," he murmured, then reached around to stroke Grady's dick to distract him from the discomfort.

"I want you," Grady said, breathless.

"Need to get you ready." When the muscles released enough to allow a single digit to move in and out, he lubed up another and added it, hearing Grady hiss at the burn. He twisted just so and brushed across Grady's spot.

"Holy shit!" Grady reached underneath to squeeze himself, trying to hold off. Dawson seized the distraction to scissor his fingers, feeling the muscles give.

"Helps if you bear down. And relax." *Easier said than done.*

Dawson kept sliding his fingers in and out until he felt the pressure ease enough to work in three.

"I'm ready," Grady insisted.

"Not trying to brag, but I'm still thicker than what you've got in there now," Dawson joked, reaching around to tug on Grady's flagging cock until it stiffened.

"Please."

Dawson knew he couldn't hold out any longer, and Grady was as ready as he was going to be. "Tell me if I need to stop."

"Just fuck me, already."

"So romantic." Dawson came up on his knees behind Grady, lining his aching cock up with that tight furl. He slicked himself up, added some more lube with his fingers to ease the intrusion, and then placed his hands on Grady's hips and pushed forward.

He heard Grady's breath catch as the head pushed past the first ring of muscle, and paused, giving Grady time to adjust.

"Do it."

"I will."

Grady pushed back, impaling himself on Dawson's cock, and Dawson thrust forward, seating himself against Grady's ass. He reached around with a slicked palm and began to stroke Grady's cock.

"Move. Daw—"

Why am I not surprised he's a bossy bottom? Dawson thought, biting back a chuckle. He drew back, then slid in again, slow at first but knowing neither of them were going to last. Grady was so hot and tight, and it was *Gray*, dammit. Finally, after everything.

Grady's panting and moans made Dawson pick up speed, thrusting faster and harder. Then he shifted, just a bit, nailed that sweet spot, and heard Grady cry out as his orgasm hit.

"Come for me, Gray," Dawson murmured, as Grady's body bucked beneath him. He tightened his grip on Grady's hips and chased his own pleasure, just a few more strokes as Grady's channel tightened impossibly around his cock, and then with one final thrust, his release washed over him, powerful and consuming. He felt himself spend deep inside Grady, filling him up, marking him, claiming him.

Grady's sweat-slick body trembled, and his breath came shallow and rapid. Dawson folded over him, kissing him lightly on his shoulders, inhaling the scent of their mingled pleasure.

"I love you, Gray. Forever."

Grady managed to twist his head so that he could glimpse Dawson over his shoulder, and Dawson pressed a kiss to his lips.

"Love you too." Grady's voice, raw and utterly fucked out, sent a final thrill through Dawson's body. He slipped out carefully and gently tipped Grady onto his side. Then he leaned over the bed and grabbed his T-shirt, bringing it back to mop up the wet spot on the sheets and gently clean his lover.

Grady sprawled bonelessly, looking gloriously debauched, and utterly wanton.

"Fuck, you're beautiful," Dawson said, still a little amazed that they'd finally made it this far.

"C'mere," Grady murmured.

Dawson tossed the T-shirt onto the floor and slid up against Grady, who wriggled down just enough to rest his head against Dawson's shoulder. Dawson brought his arm up around him, while his right hand petted Grady's hair, still feeling too mind-blown to speak.

"You okay?" he finally asked.

"Mm-hm," Grady hummed against his chest.

"You know, we can switch it up if you want," Dawson said. "I like it both ways." Truthfully, he'd rarely trusted anyone enough to bottom, but with Grady, it was different.

"Let me...catch my breath," Grady sounded barely awake.

"No hurry," Dawson assured him, squeezing his eyes closed against the emotions that threatened to overwhelm him. "Not going anywhere." A few minutes later, Grady's breathing changed, and his body relaxed.

Dawson stayed awake for a while, marveling in having Grady's naked body pressed against his, legs tangled together, Grady's hand splayed against his chest. He kissed the top of Grady's head. "Not going anywhere without you, ever again," he whispered.

———

"Nice of you to finally come home," Denny said as Dawson and Grady trooped into the house a few days later. "Enjoy your little vacay?" That last word positively dripped with sarcasm.

"Actually, yes," Dawson replied, as his hand found Grady's. Angel came running, tail wagging, and thoroughly sniffed them both, then plunked himself down in front of them to be petted.

"Good for you. It's about time. Spare me the details."

"I let the shop know we'd both work extra shifts," Dawson added, feeling a little guilty for how much time they'd been gone, what with everything that had happened the past few weeks. Yes, as Denny kept reminding him, he and Grady were part owners. Still, he didn't want to give anyone the wrong impression. Then again, there'd been some major shit going down, most of which was now finally settled.

He knew that Grady still needed time to mourn his father. The loss might change over the course of years, but it never entirely went away. Dawson knew that from losing his own parents. Most of the time, they were a fond memory at the edge of his thoughts, and then something triggered a memory, and the pain came back, sharp and fresh. But now, neither of them had to deal with those days alone.

Dawson also knew he couldn't ignore his PTSD. He would have to deal with it at some point. For now, sleeping next to Grady, having him warm and solid and close, seemed to hold the dreams at bay for both of them.

"You timed it right for dinner," Denny told them. "Go get situated. I made chicken and dumplings, and it's almost ready." Dawson inhaled deeply, and his stomach rumbled at the aroma coming from the slow cooker on the counter.

They brought their bags in with them and headed toward the back hallway, then slowed, unsure where to go.

"Your pick," Denny said from behind them. "They've both got double beds. Fine by me—fewer sheets to wash on laundry day."

Dawson felt his ears turn red, and Grady blushed an adorable shade of pink. As great as it was to have Denny on their side, that also meant he had no illusions about what they'd be getting up to whenever the door was closed.

"Thanks," Dawson said, finding himself unusually tongue-tied. Grady echoed his comment, and they escaped into what had been Dawson's room, the one farthest from Denny's bedroom.

Now that they were back home, Dawson felt strangely awkward. The room hadn't changed, but they had.

"You know, I've been thinking," Grady said as he set his bag at the foot of the bed and sat, crossing his legs under him. "I haven't dealt with Dad's house."

Dawson hadn't given that much thought. "I always figured that you and Knox would end up selling it and splitting the money."

Grady shook his head. "Dad didn't leave it to Knox. He left it to me."

Dawson's raised eyebrow prompted Grady to go on. "I love my brother, but he's made some big mistakes, and he isn't doing very well about dealing with his shit. He won't see a therapist, won't go to rehab for his drinking problem, and sooner or later, he's going to get busted for the pain pills he's addicted to."

"I'm sorry," Dawson said, feeling a little gut-punched. He and Knox were the same age, and they'd grown up together, hunted together, until Knox's accident. He knew Knox hadn't dealt with his injury well, but that wasn't exactly uncommon among hunters. "I didn't realize it was that bad."

Grady blinked quickly, tearing up, and his voice, when he spoke again, sounded strained. "Dad knew, and he did his best to help, but Knox shut him down at every turn. I think dad was afraid that Knox was either going to get himself killed or run into trouble with the law he couldn't get out of."

"And he didn't want you to lose the house."

Grady nodded. "He had savings, and he saw a lawyer not long before he died. Set the equivalent value of the house aside in a fund for Knox so he gets a check every month, but he can't touch the principal. It isn't enough that he could completely quit working, but it's a safety net if he can't."

"And something he can't blow through."

Grady swallowed hard. "Yeah. God, I hate what's happened to him. We didn't always get along, but he's still my brother."

Dawson sat next to him and slipped an arm around Grady's shoulders. Grady leaned into him, accepting the comfort.

"At first, I couldn't deal with the thought of going through Dad's things, right after..." Grady cleared his throat. "And Denny said I could stay here. He was worried about me."

"I'm glad. It worked out."

Grady shot him a smile, even though his eyes were teary. "Yeah. It did." He gave Dawson's hand a squeeze. "Then you came home, and everything started happening, and there just wasn't time to think about it. But then I started wondering—"

Dawson found himself holding his breath. This felt so right, having Grady in his arms, being able to support him and help with the hard stuff. It didn't feel new or awkward. More like it was always meant to be.

"It's not a fancy place," Grady said, turning a little to be able to see Dawson's face. "You've been there—it's going to need some fixing up. Dad had a list of projects that didn't get finished." He sniffed back tears, but his smile held. "But the bones of the house are good, and Dad owned it outright—no mortgage, no liens. So I was thinking... maybe you could move in with me?" His confidence faltered a little on that last word, and Dawson saw the question in Grady's eyes.

"Yes. Did you really think I wouldn't?" Dawson touched Grady's face with his fingertips, and Grady turned his head to press a kiss to his palm.

"Didn't want to assume. You know, we just slept together—finally —and now I'm asking you to move in with me."

Dawson rolled his eyes. "Not like we haven't known each other our whole lives."

"Still."

"The answer is yes," Dawson repeated. "That gives Denny back his privacy, and we won't have to be as quiet."

Grady's smile turned wicked. "That did cross my mind." He sighed. "We still have to clean it out, spruce things up. It could use a coat of paint. Replace a couple of appliances that aren't in great shape, that sort of thing."

"Doesn't sound like a problem. Sounds like fun." Dawson's heart sped up when he realized what Grady was asking, and he couldn't quite believe he'd gone from complete despair to finally getting his heart's desire.

"Over time, we could make it more our own," Grady went on. "But it's furnished, it's paid for, the taxes aren't bad, and there's a nice yard in the back."

"You don't have to sell me on it," Dawson chuckled. "As long as we're together. The rest, we can deal with."

Grady stretched up to kiss him, slow and sweet, but full of emotion. "Thank you."

"It's your house—pretty sure I should be thanking you."

"*Our* house."

"I like the sound of that."

They headed out to the kitchen, and Dawson felt as if one more piece had fallen into place between them. Denny ladled out bowls for Grady to put on the table, while Dawson filled water glasses and then carried over the bread, butter, and salad.

"I heard a rumor that the partner of the witch who sent the werewolf that killed Aaron went missing," Denny said after they had been eating for a while. Grady and Dawson exchanged a look.

"I'm not going to lose any sleep over it, but that's the sort of thing that can come back to bite you on the ass, if you know what I mean."

Dawson cleared his throat. "I'm sure it's taken care of." Explaining both a bullet and a stake to the heart wasn't going to go over well with the cops. Grady and Dawson had put Franco back in his fancy BMW, wiped down all the prints and removed the bullet, and then nudged it over one of the steep cliffs on a blind curve. If anyone found the wreck, there wouldn't be much of Franco left to autopsy.

"It better be." Denny fixed them both with a glare.

"It is," Dawson assured him.

"Good." Denny ate a few more mouthfuls before he continued. "So...you boys still planning to hunt?"

Dawson and Grady looked at each other. They hadn't talked about hunting, but they also hadn't talked about not hunting. Grady nodded. "If you want to."

Dawson searched Grady's eyes for any hint of wanting to back out. "It's what we do."

Grady took his hand under the table. "It's what *Kings* do." It sounded to Dawson like Grady had finally accepted that the two of them were truly together.

"Y'all are so sweet it's making my teeth hurt," Denny growled, but a twinkle in his eyes softened his tone. "Is that a yes?"

"I think it's a hell, yes," Dawson replied.

"Good. Because once you two love birds are settled, I've got a hunt for you."

Dawson grinned as Grady squeezed his hand, and Dawson realized that he finally felt like he was exactly where he needed to be. "Then go ahead and tell us all about it—after dessert."

AFTERWORD

Kings of the Mountain draws on so many things that are near to my heart. I love the mountains of North Carolina and am intrigued by the large forests where with a little imagination, anything could happen, and any creatures might be hiding. I've loved ghost stories and reading about cryptids and monsters since I was little, and those tales have always fueled my imagination. One of my favorite parts of research is delving into the "lore"—folklore, mythology, and urban legends to find just the right pieces to root a story in its location.

If you've read my other Morgan Brice books, you know that sooner or later, all of my series cross over with each other, and with the urban fantasy I write as Gail Z. Martin. If you're wondering about the guy Denny knew in Myrtle Beach who was good with lore, that's Simon Kincaide, one of the main characters in my Badlands series. As the Kings of the Mountain series goes on, I'm sure there will be many more tie-ins and character appearances. After all, the monster hunting community is fairly small, so it makes sense for the people in it to know each other and help each other out.

Stay tuned—Dawson and Grady will be back with more adventures!

ACKNOWLEDGMENTS

It takes a village to get a book out into the world. As always, I want to thank my husband, Larry N. Martin, for all his behind-the-scenes work with brainstorming, editing, formatting, tracking, uploading, and so many other things that go into this crazy business of writing. Of course, there's also our editor, Jean Rabe, our cover artist, Natania Barron, and the wonderfully supportive readers in my Worlds of Morgan Brice group and my Shadow Alliance group, as well as the Spookies in Reading Past The Realm. A huge "I luv you" goes out to all my readers everywhere! Because you read, I write.

I can't say "thank you" enough to my wonderful beta and ARC readers, including: Amy, Andrea, Anne, Anthony, Barbara, Belinda, Beth, Carole, Carrah, Cheryl, Chris, Cindi, Danae, Darrell, Debbie, Diane, Dino, Elayne, Eleanor, Elle, Gabby, George, Grace, Ida, Jennifer, Karolina, Laurie, Lexi, Lisa, Liz, Manda, Mandy, Mindy, Olga, Patricia, Patti, Pavel, Rita, Sandra, Sharon, Stacy, Suzanne, Terri, Wendy, and Xochitl for their awesome help in getting the book into its best final form and letting the world know. Thank you also to Andrea, Leslie, and Mud for their help, and to all my marketing partners, as well as the amazing bloggers and reviewers, and the wonderful fellow authors who have been so generous with their advice and support. Also thanks to Kipp and Flynn, our dogs, for their patience and cuddles.

ALSO BY MORGAN BRICE

Witchbane Series

Witchbane

Burn, a Witchbane Novella

Dark Rivers

Flame and Ash

Unholy

Badlands Series

Badlands

Restless Nights, a Badlands Short Story

Lucky Town, a Badlands Novella

The Rising

Cover Me, a Badlands Short Story

Loose Ends

Leap of Faith, A Badlands/Witchbane Novella

Night, a Badlands Short Story

Treasure Trail Series

Treasure Trail

Kings of the Mountain Series

Kings of the Mountain

ABOUT THE AUTHOR

Morgan Brice is the romance pen name of bestselling author Gail Z. Martin. Morgan writes urban fantasy male/male paranormal romance, with plenty of action, adventure, and supernatural thrills to go with the happily ever after.

Gail writes epic fantasy and urban fantasy, and together with co-author hubby Larry N. Martin, steampunk and comedic horror, all of which have less romance and more explosions.

On the rare occasions Morgan isn't writing, she's either reading, cooking, or spoiling two very pampered dogs.

Watch for additional new series from Morgan Brice, and more books in the Witchbane, Badlands, and Treasure Trail universes coming soon!

Where to find me, and how to stay in touch

Join my Worlds of Morgan Brice Facebook Group and get in on all the behind-the-scenes fun! My free reader group is the first to see cover reveals, learn tidbits about works-in-progress, have fun with exclusive contests and giveaways, find out about in-person get-togethers, and more! It's also where I find my beta readers, ARC readers and launch team! Come join the party! www.Facebook.com/groups/WorldsOfMorganBrice

Find me on the web at https://morganbrice.com. Sign up for my newsletter and never miss a new release! http://eepurl.com/dy_8oL. You can also find me on Twitter: @MorganBriceBook, on Pinterest (for Morgan and Gail): pinterest.com/Gzmartin, on Instagram as

MorganBriceAuthor, and on Bookbub https://www.bookbub.com/authors/morgan-brice

Enjoy two free short stories set in my Badlands series. Read *Cover Me* here for free: https://claims.prolificworks.com/free/iwZDEP9Z and *Restless Nights* here: https://claims.prolificworks.com/free/js6xofq8

Come check out the ongoing, online convention ConTinual www.facebook.com/groups/ConTinual

Support Indie Authors

When you support independent authors, you help influence what kind of books you'll see more of and what types of stories will be available, because the authors themselves decide which books to write, not a big publishing conglomerate. Independent authors are local creators, supporting their families with the books they produce. Thank you for supporting independent authors and small press fiction!